21**世纪高等学校规划教材**

DAXUE YINGYU SHIYONG JIAOCHENG (1)

大学英语实用教程(1)

主　编　刘新华
副主编　徐莉芳　陈永生　段雪芹
参　编　张秀菊　杨慧　周军
主　审　Dewan Benjamin

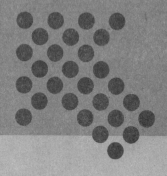

中国电力出版社
http://jc.cepp.com.cn

内 容 提 要

本书为 21 世纪高等学校规划教材。

《大学英语实用教程》共分四册，每册都以对话、课文及语法三部分形式表现，内容新颖实用、条理清晰、通俗易懂、针对性强。本书为第一册，重点为词的讲练。在每单元里采用一个主题，分别用对话和课文的形式来培养学生的听、说、读、写、译全方位的实际表达技能。在语法部分中，以非英语专业学位考试大纲要求为主线，更加注重实用性和针对性。每单元之间既相互独立又互相呼应，且单元中的对话、课文、语法都配有相应的习题及参考答案。

本书可作为高等院校非英语专业教材，也可作为高职高专院校及远程教育、业大、函授等学生的基础英语课教材，并可作为成人非英语专业学位考试的参考用书。

图书在版编目（CIP）数据

大学英语实用教程（1）/ 刘新华主编. —北京：中国电力出版社，2009

21 世纪高等学校规划教材

ISBN 978-7-5083-8308-8

Ⅰ. 大⋯　Ⅱ. 刘⋯　Ⅲ. 英语－高等学校－教材　Ⅳ. H31

中国版本图书馆 CIP 数据核字（2008）第 212030 号

中国电力出版社出版、发行

（北京三里河路 6 号　100044　http://jc.cepp.com.cn）

航远印刷有限公司印刷

各地新华书店经售

*

2009 年 2 月第一版　2009 年 2 月北京第一次印刷

787 毫米×1092 毫米　16 开本　10.75 印张　258 千字

定价 17.50 元

前　言

　　本书是 21 世纪高等学校规划教材，内容新颖实用、条理清晰、通俗易懂、针对性强，《大学英语实用教程》共分四册。每册主要由对话、课文及语法三部分组成。对话部分以提供的主题示例训练学生实际交流及表达的能力；课文部分侧重对语言点和语篇整体的理解，为非英语专业的学生在学位考试中的阅读部分打下坚实的基础；语法部分中，结合学生英语基础知识和基本能力的实际，针对非英语专业学位考试大纲要求，有的放矢。在内容上，全面覆盖考点，重点突出，系统性强；在形式上，题型新颖，利于学生能力的训练和培养；在编排上，注意由易到难的阶梯性、针对性和适用性。

　　本套教材的每个单元紧密配合，又不重复；单元内的内容又相对独立，可根据学生的实际情况调整侧重点；并且，每个单元中的对话、课文、语法三部分都配有相应的练习。

　　本书为《大学英语实用教程（1）》，作者为北京科技大学等高校的一线英语教师，他们具有丰富的教学与实践经验，以确保本套教材教学的可操作性、针对性及实用性。

　　本书由刘新华主编，徐莉芳、陈永生、段雪芹副主编，张秀菊、杨慧、周军也参加了编写工作。

　　在编写过程中，参考了大量的书籍和资料，有些内容难免引自其中，在此对原作者表示诚挚的谢意！同时对许多给予帮助与支持的同事、朋友，一并表示衷心的感谢。

　　由于编者的能力和水平有限，书中难免有不足或错误之处，恳请广大读者批评指正。

编　者

2008 年 10 月于北京科技大学

目　录

前　言

Unit 1　Students' Life 1
　Communicative Samples 1
　Paragraph Reading A: Adult Education 2
　Paragraph Reading B: How to Judge a Person 5
　Grammar Focus: General Introduction 概说 7

Unit 2　Environment & Conservation 11
　Communicative Samples 11
　Paragraph Reading A: Water Pollution 12
　Paragraph Reading B: Nature Conservation 15
　Grammar Focus: Nouns 名词 17

Unit 3　Web 21
　Communicative Samples 21
　Paragraph Reading A: Welcome to the Web! 22
　Paragraph Reading B: Ready, Steady, Go! 25
　Grammar Focus: Articles 冠词 27

Unit 4　Climate & Weather 32
　Communicative Samples 32
　Paragraph Reading A: How to Measure Distance in California 33
　Paragraph Reading B: Hurricane 36
　Grammar Focus: Pronouns 代词（一）... 38

Unit 5　Culture 42
　Communicative Samples 42
　Paragraph Reading A: Father's Day 43
　Paragraph Reading B: Holidays & Vacation 46
　Grammar Focus: Pronoun 代词（二）.. 48

Unit 6　Sports & Games 52
　Communicative Samples 52
　Paragraph Reading A: Jesse Owens 53
　Paragraph Reading B: Sports 55
　Grammar Focus: Number 数词 58

Unit 7　People's Life 62
　Communicative Samples 62
　Paragraph Reading A: Fire Disaster 63

Paragraph Reading B: Hawaii 65

Grammar Focus: Preposition 介词 68

Unit 8   Studying Online 72

Communicative Samples 72

Paragraph Reading A: Internet 73

Paragraph Reading B: How to Read 75

Grammar Focus: Adjective & Adverb 形容词和副词（一）...................... 78

Unit 9   Traffic & Transmission 82

Communicative Samples 82

Paragraph Reading A: The Trans-Amazonian Highway 83

Paragraph Reading B: Asking for a Way 86

Grammar Focus: Adjective & Adverb 形容词和副词（二）...................... 88

Unit 10   Letters 92

Communicative Samples 92

Paragraph Reading A: Pen Friends 93

Paragraph Reading B：Fun at the Supermarket 96

Grammar Focus: Tense 时态（一）... 98

Unit 11   Energy Resources 102

Communicative Samples 102

Paragraph Reading A: Recycling Waste 103

Paragraph Reading B: How to Solve the Energy Shortage........................ 106

Grammar Focus: Tense 时态（二）... 108

Unit 12   How to Learn 112

Communicative Samples 112

Paragraph Reading A: Vast, West or Vest 113

Paragraph Reading B: Marking on Books 116

Grammar Focus: Tense 时态（三）.. 118

Glossary 122

Model Test 1 136

Model Test 2 146

Answer Keys 155

Unit 1   Students' Life
Communicative Samples

Conversation 1

(Wang Li and Karen have just finished class and are going to lunch.)

Wang Li: Oh, the class is finally dismissed.

Karen: Yes. Mr. Smith's lecture almost made me fall into sleep.

Wang Li: Do you like English classes?

Karen: I like English classes, but I don't like memorizing the English words.

Wang Li: Which canteen do you prefer?

Karen: I usually prefer canteen No.3. And you?

Wang Li: Me, too. I'll go to the canteen with you.

(They get to the canteen.)

Wang Li: The food smells good. I think I'm going to guite a lot.

Karen: You always order more than you need.

Wang Li: The stewed cabbage with beef looks good. Why not try some?

Karen: You're right. It does look good. I think I will.

Conversation 2

(Two students are talking about classes.)

McKee: Hi, David. Have you decided what classes you will take next semester?

David: No, I'm not sure yet. I was thinking about taking some art classes.

McKee: Are you majoring in art?

David: No, I major in English, but I am very interested in art.

McKee: What kind of art are you interested in?

David: Oh，anything. Right now I don't know much, so I will take some basic classes. What is your major?

McKee: I am majoring in mathematics.

David: That sounds very difficult. Is it?

McKee: Yes, it is. I have to study very hard. I have no time for having fun.

David: I don't think I would like that. I was never very good at mathematics.

McKee: Well, class will start soon, so I must go now. See you later.

David: Bye.

New Words and Expressions

dismiss	/dis'mis/	v.	解散，开除
lecture	/'lektʃə/	n. & v.	演讲
canteen	/kæn'tiːn/	n.	食堂，餐厅
cabbage	/'kæbidʒ/	n.	卷心菜
beef	/biːf/	n.	牛肉
semester	/si'mestə/	n.	学期
major	/'meidʒə/	n. v. & adj.	主修课，主修，主要的
mathematics	/ˌmæθi'mætiks/	n.	数学

Exercise 1: Complete the following sentences.

A: Hi，David. _____ (你主修什么)?

B: I am majoring in mathematics. How about you?

A: _____ (我主修英语).

B: Really? Good major.

A: Yes. _____ (我觉得英语特别有趣).

B: I think so.

Exercise 2: Fill in the missing letters.

dismi_ _　　　l_ _ture　　　can_ _en　　　st_ _　　　c_ _ba _e

b_ _f　　　w_ _der_ _ _　　　s_ _e_t_ _　　　m_j_ _　　　ma_ _em_t_ _s

Paragraph Reading A: Adult Education

Millions of people are enrolled in evening adult education programs across America. Community colleges have become popular and their enrollments have increased rapidly. Large universities are offering more courses in the evening for adult students. In this way, the demand for more education is being met. One reason for this is that many elder people are changing their professions. They are looking for different careers. Another reason is that repair costs have increased. Adults are taking courses like pluming and electrical repair. This way they hope that the high costs for repairs can be avoided. Advanced technology is the most important reason for the rise in adult education. Engineers, teachers and businessmen are taking adult education classes. They have found that more education is needed to do their jobs well. Various courses are offered. Computer and business courses are taken by many adult students. Foreign languages, accounting and communication courses are also popular. Some students attend classes to earn degrees. Others take courses for the knowledge and skills that they can receive. The lives of many people have been enriched because of adult education.

New Words and Expressions

adult	/əˈdʌlt/	n. & adj.	成人，成人的
community	/kəˈmjuːniti/	n.	团体，社会
enrollment	/inˈrəulmənt/	n.	注册
rapidly	/ˈræpidli/	adv.	迅速地
demand	/diˈmɑːnd/	n. & v.	要求
education	/ˌedju(ː)ˈkeiʃən/	n.	教育
change	/tʃeindʒ/	n. & vt.	变化，改变
profession	/prəˈfeʃən/	n.	职业，专业
career	/kəˈriə/	n.	事业，生涯
pluming	/plʌmiŋ/	n.	（建筑物的）管路系统；自来水管道
electrical	/iˈlektrik(ə)l/	adj.	电的，与电有关的
avoid	/əˈvɔid/	vt.	避免
technology	/tekˈnɔlədʒi/	n.	科技，技术
various	/ˈvɛəriəs/	adj.	各种各样的
accounting	/əˈkauntiŋ/	n.	会计学
degree	/diˈgriː/	n.	学位，度
knowledge	/ˈnɔlidʒ/	n.	知识
enrich	/inˈritʃ/	vt.	使丰富

Exercise 3:   Select the answer that best expresses the main idea of the paragraph reading A.

1) One can take adult education courses_____.

    A. in a private college or university   B. at home

    C. at his (or her) working place   D. in a community college or university

2) Adult education has become popular_____.

    A. because many old people are changing their professions

    B. because some people are looking for better jobs

    C. because they have high costs for repairs and advanced technology

    D. all of the above

3) Generally_____.

    A. large universities are offering much help for us students

    B. universities are giving more courses during the daytime

    C. universities are not giving courses in the evening for adult students

    D. large universities are giving courses in the evening for adult students

4) Which of the following courses is not offered in evening adult education programs?

A. pluming and electrical repair　　　B. engineering

C. foreign languages　　　D. accounting and communication

5) Which of the following statements is not true according to the selection?

A. People go to attend the evening adult classes for more money.

B. They go there because they want to enrich their lives.

C. They have to study more because of the advanced technology.

D. They do so for the reason that they want to do jobs better.

Exercise 4: Fill in the blanks with words and expressions given below. Change the form where necessary.

skill	various	look for	profession	degree	avoid	electrical	increase
attend	demand	enroll	in this way	communication		receive	career

1) Mr. Smith has _____ her daughter in the drawing class.

2) The gross national product had _____ 5 percent last year.

3) Why do you represent the matter _____?

4) This work _____ your immediate attention.

5) Nursing is a vocation as well as a _____.

6) He began to _____ another position immediately.

7) His early _____ was not a great success.

8) Now _____ appliances have entered into ordinary families.

9) To _____ the city center, turn right here.

10) For _____ reasons I'd prefer not to meet him.

11) This area has not been covered by the _____ net.

12) Danger _____ everything he did.

13) We can only make progress by _____.

14) The crisis put his courage and _____ to the test.

15) He was _____ as an honored visitor.

Exercise 5: Definitions of these words appear on the right. Put the letter of the appropriate definition next to each word.

1) _____ education　　　a. profession

2) _____ career　　　b. keep or get away from

3) _____ avoid　　　c. person or animal grown to full size and strength

4) _____ knowledge　　　d. systematic training and instruction

5) _____ adult　　　e. range of information

Exercise 6: Translate the following short passage.

For those students who took part in and passed fair examinations, it is unfair if some of them cannot enter into colleges because of economic reasons. At present, a reasonable and effective way to solve college students' economic problems has not been found yet. Higher education fees have been increasing every year. In such condition it is impossible for students from low-income families or the countryside to afford college study.

Paragraph Reading B: How to Judge a Person

Have you ever heard the old saying "Never judge a book by its cover"? This is a good rule to follow when trying to judge the intelligence of others. Some people have minds that shine only in certain situations. A young man with an unusual gift in writing may find himself speechless before a pretty girl when he speaks. He may not be able to find the right words. But don't make the mistake of thinking

him stupid. With a pen and paper, he can express himself better than anybody else.

Other people may fool you into overestimating their intelligence by putting up a good front. A student who listens attentively and takes notes in class is bound to make a favorable impression on his teachers, but when it comes to exams, he may score near the bottom of the class.

In a word, you can't judge someone by appearance. The only way to determine a person's intelligence is to get to know him. Then you can see how he reacts to different situations. The more situations you see, the better your judgment is likely to be. So take your time. Don't judge a book by its cover.

New Words and Expressions

judge	/dʒʌdʒ/	*n. & v.*	判断
cover	/ˈkʌvə/	*n. & v.*	封面，覆盖
intelligence	/inˈtelidʒəns/	*n.*	智力
shine	/ʃain/	*n. & v.*	光亮，发光
situation	/ˌsitjuˈeiʃən/	*n.*	情形
unusual	/ʌnˈjuːʒuəl/	*adj.*	不平常的
speechless	/ˈspiːtʃlis/	*adj.*	不能说话的
mistake	/misˈteik/	*n. & v.*	错误；犯错，弄错
stupid	/ˈstjuːpid/	*adj.*	愚蠢的
express	/iksˈpres/	*n. & v.*	表达
else	/els/	*adj. & adv.*	其他的
fool	/fuːl/	*n. v. & adj.*	蠢人；愚蠢的
overestimate	/ˈəuvəˈestimeit/	*n. & v.*	评价过高
frond	/frɔnd/	*n.*	叶，植物体

attentively	/ə'tentivli/	adv.	注意地
bound	/baund/	adj.	一定会，很可能会
favorable	/'feivərəbl/	adj.	赞成的，有利的
impression	/im'preʃən/	n.	印象
score	/skɔː/	n. & v.	计分，得分
appearance	/ə'piərəns/	n.	外貌，外观
determine	/di'təːmin/	v.	决定
react	/ri'ækt/	vi.	起反应

Exercise 7: Select the answer that best expresses the main idea of the paragraph reading B.

1) The passage suggests that _____.
   A. a good writer may not be a good speaker
   B. a good writer is always a good speaker
   C. a speechless person always writes well
   D. a good writer will find himself speechless

2) According to this passage, a student who listens attentively and takes notes in class _____.
   A. is an intelligent student
   B. may not be an intelligent student
   C. will score better in exams
   D. will not be a good student

3) The passage suggests that we should judge a person's intelligence through _____.
   A. his teachers
   B. his deeds in the classroom
   C. his appearance
   D. his reactions to different situations

4) The writer in this passage wants to tell us not to _____.
   A. judge a book by its cover
   B. make the mistake of thinking a young man stupid
   C. overestimate a student's intelligence
   D. judge a person's intelligence by his appearance

5) Which words a young man may not be able to find?
   A. correctly   B. satisfactory
   C. well   D. truly

Exercise 8: Fill in the blanks with words and expressions given below. Change the form where necessary.

| get to know appearance cover try to intelligence shine situation bottom |
| pretty take your time bound to overestimate favorable judgment make mistake |

1) We tried to find _____ from the storm.
2) Even when you argue, you should _____ keep cool.

3) He equals me in strength but not in _____.

4) I hate lights being _____ in my face.

5) The company is in a poor financial _____.

6) What a _____ little garden!

7) You _____ if you do things in a hurry.

8) I _____ his abilities he's finding the job very difficult.

9) I am _____ say I disagree with you on this point.

10) Most people were _____ to the idea.

11) He was always _____ of the class in maths.

12) I don't want to go to the party but I'd better put in an _____, I suppose.

13) How did you _____ that I was here?

14) Her decision seems to show a lack of political _____.

15) It's an important decision for you, so _____ to think it over.

Exercise 9: Definitions of these words appear on the right. Put the letter of the appropriate definition next to each word.

1) _____ frond   a. guard from attack

2) _____ situation   b. a large leaf especially of a fern or palm tree

3) _____ mistake   c. understand wrongly

4) _____ cover   d. the way in which something is placed in relation to its surroundings

5) _____ impression   e. the act or process of impressing

Grammar Focus: General Introduction 概说

一、词的分类

英语中的单词可以根据词义、句法作用和形式特征，分为十大类：

词　类	作　用	例　词
名词 Noun (n.)	表示人或事物的名称	student Internet
代词 Pronoun (pron.)	代替名词、数词等	we she
动词 Verb (v.)	表示动作或状态	fight know
形容词 Adjective (adj.)	表示人或事物的特征	happy clean
副词 Adverb (adv.)	表示动作特征或性状特征	very hardly
数词 Numeral (num.)	表示数目或顺序	seven third
冠词 Article (art.)	用在名词前，帮助说明其含义	a (an) the

词　类	作　用	例　词
介词 Preposition (prep.)	用在名词、代词前，说明它与别的词的关系	with by
连词 Conjunction (conj.)	用来连接词和词或句与句	and if
感叹词 Interjection (int.)	表示说话时的感情或语气	oh ah

以上十种词类中，前六种可以在句子中独立担任成分，称为实义词，而后四种都不能在句子中独立担任任何成分，称为虚词。

分清词类很重要，不同的词类之间有不同的关系，同时也担任不同的句子成分。

二、词类相互间的关系

（1）形容词、数词通常修饰名词，形容词还可修饰代词。

e.g. The three tall men are all soccer players.

（数词 three 和形容词 tall 修饰名词 men）

He often writes something interesting in his diary.

（形容词 interesting 修饰不定代词 something）

（2）副词常修饰动词、形容词和副词。

e.g. Miss Liu plays the piano quite well.

（副词 well 修饰动词 plays，副词 quite 修饰另一副词 well）

The news is very instructive.

（副词 very 修饰形容词 instructive）

（3）冠词、介词、连接词和感叹词是虚词，在句中不能单独构成句子成分，只起辅助和连接的作用。

冠词只用于名词之前，辅助指明名词的含义。

介词与它后面的名词或代词构成介词短语时，才能在句中作定语、状语和表语。

连词起连接词、词组和句子的作用。

感叹词可看作特殊的一类，一般放在句首。

三、词类和句子成分的关系

句子是由作用不同的各部分组成的，这些部分就叫做句子成分。句子成分可以是单词，也可以是词组或从句。

在句子中起主要作用的句子成分有主语、谓语，称为主要成分；起次要作用的有宾语、宾语补足语、定语、状语、表语等，称为次要成分。

（1）主语是句子要说明的人或物，是句子的主体，通常放在句首。一般由名词或起名词作用的其他词类、短语或从句担任。

e.g. **Mr. Smith** is a well-known musician.（名词作主语）

Smoking is harmful to health.（动名词作主语）

What we are going to do has not been decided yet.（从句作主语）

（2）谓语是说明主语的动作或状态。动词在句中作谓语，一般放在主语之后。

e.g. The new term **begins** on September 1st.（行为动词）

She **seems** tired.（系动词）

（3）宾语一般用在及物动词的后面，表示行为或对象的结果，称为动词宾语；介词后面的名词或代词称为介词宾语。名词、代词、数词常作宾语。

e.g. We love **China**.（动词宾语）

The medicine is good for **a cough**.（介词宾语）

（4）表语在系动词后用来说明主语的身份、状态或特征。可作表语的有名词、代词、形容词和表语从句等。

e.g. She is always **careless**.（形容词作表语）

The question is **we don't know the answer**.（从句作表语）

（5）定语用来修饰名词或代词。形容词、数词和定语从句等都可作定语。

e.g. I have something **important** to tell you.（形容词作定语）

This is the new computer **which I bought yesterday**.（从句作定语）

（6）状语是修饰动词、形容词、副词或全句的成分的。副词、介词词组、名词词组和状语从句等都可以作状语。

e.g. He sings **quite well**.（副词作状语）

We will leave for Japan **the day after tomorrow**.（名词词组作状语）

If I have some spare time, I want to learn cooking.（从句作状语）

Exercise 10: 写出下列句中斜体单词的词义、词类及在句中的作用。

1) Please *close* the window before you leave.

2) I forgot to repair my *watch*.

3) She will go to Nanjing by a *fast* train.

4) Don't speak to me *like* that.

5) Keep *quiet* when you read in the library.

6) Though the *work* is not easy he loves it very much.

Exercise 11: 将下列句子译成汉语并分析句子成分。

1) Time flies fast.

2) I am in a hurry to find a job.

3) Can you get him to help me?

4) The people all over the world are hoping for peace.

5) He bought some sweets for his son.

6) You had better answer the question in English.

Unit 2　Environment & Conservation
Communicative Samples

Conversation 1

(Two friends are talking about the very serious water pollution.)

Jim:　　I remember we could swim in the river fifteen years ago.

Kevin: Yes. But now, it is dangerous.

Jim:　　That's terrible. The water is becoming polluted.

Kevin: Yes. The pollution can kill fish and make the water bad.

Jim:　　Polluted water does harm to everyone.

Kevin: The quality of ground water is getting worse and worse.

Jim:　　If the water gets worse, we'll face with a drinking water crisis.

Kevin: That's all right.

Jim:　　And I think we can do something to reduce pollution if we work hard together.

Kevin: How can people deal with the waste water?

Jim:　　Cities should be built sewage-treatment factories so that we can reuse the water.

Kevin: Let's work together for a better world.

Conversation 2

(Tom is fishing with his father.)

Tom:　　Dad, what's that thick black thing in the river?

Father: That's the waste from some factories.

Tom:　　Then the river is polluted.

Father: Not only the rivers, but also the air and the soil.

Tom:　　The air is also polluted?

Father: Don't you see so many people cough day and night? Do your eyes fill with tears when you are near the factory?

Tom:　　Yes, they do but I don't know why.

Father: Because there is too much sulfur dioxide in the air.

Tom:　　What should we do?

Father: Perhaps next time when we come fishing, we need some masks.

New Words and Expressions

pollution	/pəˈluːʃən/	n.	污染
harm	/hɑːm/	n. & v.	伤害
underground	/ˈʌndəgraund/	n. & adj.	地铁，地下的
crisis	/ˈkraisis/	n.	危机
garbage	/ˈgɑːbidʒ/	n.	垃圾
sewage-treatment	/ˈsjuː(ː)idʒ/		污水处理
stream	/striːm/	n. & v.	溪，流
sulfur	/ˈsʌlfə/	n. & v.	硫磺；用硫磺处理
dioxide	/daiˈɔksaid/	n.	二氧化物
mask	/mɑːsk/	n.	面具

Exercise 1: Complete the following sentences.

A: Tom, do you know that water pollution is a serious problem?

B: _____ (是的).

A: _____ (受到污染的水对人类是有害的).

B: Yes. How do we protect our water resources?

A: We can _____ (减少水污染).

B: You're absolutely right.

Exercise 2: Fill in the missing letters.

cr_ _k   p_lluti_ _   h_z_ _d   qu_ _i_y   c_ _sis

g_ _b_ _ _   str_ _m   f_ _m   s_lf_ _   d_ _xi_ _

Paragraph Reading A: Water Pollution

Water pollution is caused by waste from factories and cities. Oceans are able to clean themselves, but certain seas, once they become dirty, and not able to do so. One example is the Mediterranean which lies between Europe and Africa. It has only one narrow entrance to the ocean on its western side. One quarter of the shores of the Mediterranean is polluted and is no longer safe for swimming as a lot of diseases are present in the water. In most places it is not safe to eat the fish.

Lakes also have the same problems. Lake Baikal in Asia was once the cleanest in the world, with over 700 different kinds of plant and animal life. Now, however, the water of this great lake, which is also the world's deepest (over 1,740

metres), have been dirtied by waste from a chemical factory.

In 1989 an oil tanker hit a rock off the northwest coast of Alaska. 35,000 tons of oil poured into the sea. The accident was one of the worst in history. More than 34,000 birds and 10,000 animals were killed. 4,800 square kilometers of ocean were polluted.

New Words and Expressions

cause	/kɔːz/	n. & v.	原因
waste	/weist/	n.& v.	废物
dirty	/ˈdəːti/	v. & adj.	弄脏，脏的
example	/igˈzɑːmpl/	n.	例子
Mediterranean	/ˌmeditəˈreinjən/	n. & adj.	地中海
Europe	/ˈjuərəp/	n.	欧洲
Africa	/ˈæfrikə/	n.	非洲
narrow	/ˈnærəu/	n. & v.	窄的
entrance	/ˈentrəns/	n.	入口
quarter	/ˈkwɔːtə/	n.	四分之一
safe	/seif/	n. & adj.	安全，安全的
disease	/diˈziːz/	n.	疾病
problem	/ˈprɔbləm/	n.	问题
animal	/ˈæniməl/	n.	动物
chemical	/ˈkemikəl/	adj.	化学的
rock	/rɔk/	n. & v.	岩石，摇动
Alaska	/əˈlæskə/	n.	阿拉斯加州
pour	/pɔː/	v.	倾泻
accident	/ˈæksidənt/	n.	事故
kill	/kil/	v.	杀死
square	/skwɛə/	n.	（用于数字的表示面积）平方

Exercise 3: Select the answer that best expresses the main idea of the paragraph reading A.

1) What does the paragraph state?

   A. Lake Baikal has been polluted by waste from a chemical factory.

   B. It is no longer safe to swim in the water.

   C. Water pollution is a serious problem.

   D. An oil tanker hit a rock off the northwest coast in 1989.

2) In the first paragraph, the word "diseases" refers to _____.

   A. sharks   B. fishes

   C. illness   D. crocodile

　3) What is the difference between oceans and certain seas?

　　A. Oceans are bigger than some certain seas.

　　B. Oceans are able to clean themselves, but certain seas cannot.

　　C. Certain seas are clean, but oceans are very dirty.

　　D. It is safe to eat fish in oceans.

　4) Why is it not safe for swimmers when the water is polluted?

　　A. Because water is not able to clean itself once they become dirty.

　　B. Because there are lots of sharks in the water.

　　C. Because nobody likes swimming in the river.

　　D. Because there are a lot of diseases in the water.

　5) The author states all the following except that _____.

　　A. In 1989 an oil tanker hit a rock off the northwest coast of Alaska

　　B. Lake Baikal has been polluted by waste from a chemical factory and cities

　　C. Water pollution is caused by waste from factories and cities

　　D. Lake Baikal in Asia is the cleanest in the world

Exercise 4: Fill in the blanks with words and expressions given below. Change the form where necessary.

| at present | pollution | square | certain | dirty | coast | narrow | quarter |
| no longer | waste | chemical | pour into | disease | accident | entrance |

　1) It will cause _____ and the destruction of our seas and oceans.

　2) I can't say for _____ when he will arrive.

　3) Repairing cars is a _____ work.

　4) They planned to _____ the gap between imports and exports.

　5) I'll meet you at the _____ of the zoo tomorrow.

　6) The clock strikes the hours, the half-hours and the _____.

　7) This word is _____ in current use.

　8) The poor man has a serious _____ of the liver.

　9) I'm afraid I can't help you, but _____ I'm too busy.

　10) It's only a _____ of time to speak to her.

　11) My major is the subject of _____ engineering.

　12) He is going to live by the _____ for the sake of his health.

　13) Commuters were _____ the station.

　14) His left knee was hurt in a traffic _____.

　15) The little girl drew a _____ on the paper.

Exercise 5: Definitions of these words appear on the right. Put the letter of the appropriate definition next to each word.

　1) _____ accident　　　　　　a. something or someone that brings about a result

　2) _____ cause　　　　　　　b. the action of polluting

3) _____ disease　　　　　c. an abnormal bodily condition of a living plant or animal

4) _____ pollution　　　　　d. acted or operated or produced by chemicals

5) _____ chemical　　　　　e. an event occurs by chance

Exercise 6: Translate the following sentences.

Do you think that by staying at home you are safe from all the terrible kinds of pollution present outdoors? Do you think that by staying in your office you are breathing cleaner, safer air than when you go outside for lunch or are on the way back home from work? In fact, staying indoors may actually be more harmful to one's health than being outdoors even in soggy cities. Apparently, we are safe neither at home nor in the business office.

Paragraph Reading B: Nature Conservation

1970 was "World Conservation Year". The United Nations wanted everyone to know that the world is in danger. They hoped that government would act quickly in order to conserve nature. Here is one example of the problem. At one time there were 1,300 different plants, trees and flowers in Holland, but now only 860 remain. The others have been destroyed by modern man and his technology. We are changing the earth, the air and the water, and everything that grows and lives. We can't live without these things. If we continue like this, we shall destroy ourselves.

What will happen in the future? Perhaps it is more important to ask "What must we do?" The people who will be living in the world of tomorrow are the young of today. A lot of them know that conservation is necessary. Many are helping to save our world. They plant trees in forests, build bridges across rivers and so on. In a small town in the United States a large group of girls cleaned the banks of eleven kilometers of their river. Young people may hear about conservation through a record called NO ONE'S GOING TO CHANGE OUR WORLD. It was made by the Scatles, Cliff Richard and other singers. The money from it will help to conserve wild animals.

New Words and Expressions

conservation	/ˌkɔnsə(ː)ˈveiʃən/	n.	保存
the United Nation		n.	联合国
danger	/ˈdeindʒə/	n.	危险

government	/ˈɡʌvənmənt/	n.	政府
nature	/ˈneitʃə/	n.	自然
plant	/plɑːnt/	n. & v.	植物，种植
remain	/riˈmein/	v.	保持
destroy	/disˈtrɔi/	v.	破坏
modern	/ˈmɔdən/	adj.	现代的
continue	/kənˈtinjuː/	v.	继续
future	/ˈfjuːtʃə/	n. & adj.	未来
necessary	/ˈnesisəri/	n. & adj.	必需品，必需的
bridge	/bridʒ/	n.	桥
forest	/ˈfɔrist/	n.	森林
record	/ˈrekɔːd/	n. & v.	报告，记录
money	/ˈmʌni/	n.	钱

Exercise 7: Select the answer that best expresses the main idea of the paragraph reading B.

1) This passage is mainly about conserving _____.

    A. wild animals   B. wild plants   C. nature   D. man

2) How many kinds of plants, trees and flowers have been destroyed by modern man and his technology in Holland?

    A. 1,300   B. 860   C. 440   D. 1,000

3) We know from the passage that there are _____.

    A. more trees in Holland now   B. more flowers in Holland now

    C. fewer plants in Holland now   D. fewer animals in Holland now

4) What does the underlined word "them" refer to?

    A. all the people   B. old people

    C. old and young people   D. young people

5) We can guess from the passage that "NO ONE'S GOING TO CHANGE OUR WORLD" was _____.

    A. a book about saving the earth

    B. a song loved by young people

    C. a film about protecting wild animals

    D. a tape of songs calling on people to conserve nature

Exercise 8: Fill in the blanks with words and expressions given below. Change the form where necessary.

| continue | in danger | help to | government | conserve | clean | remain | destroy |
| kilometer | modern | happen | bridge | hear | | singer | technology |

1) You are _____ of catching a cold if you don't take any medicine.

2) The _____ would not even consider his claim for money.

3) We must _____ our forests and woodlands for future generations.

4) When the others had gone, Mary _____ and put back the furniture.

5) The fighter plane was completely _____.

6) He can't adjust himself to the whirl of _____ life in this big city.

7) The results of this research can be applied to new developments in _____.

8) The desert _____ as far as the eye could see.

9) I _____ on just the thing I'd been looking for.

10) The _____ is not strong enough to allow the passage of vehicles.

11) Please _____ the window as I can hardly see out.

12) The farm is about 50 or 60 square _____ in the area.

13) We listened but could _____ nothing.

14) The _____ devoted his whole life to the study of the songs in the northwest part of China.

15) We need _____ to get the wheat in.

Exercise 9: Definitions of these words appear on the right. Put the letter of the appropriate definition next to each word.

1) _____ nature   a. natural scenery

2) _____ forest   b. going to happen with no way of preventing it

3) _____ destroy   c. a dense growth of trees and underbrush covering a large area

4) _____ necessary   d. to put an end to; do away with

5) _____ government   e. the act or process of governing

Grammar Focus: Nouns 名词

一、名词的定义和分类

（1）定义：表示人、事物或抽象概念的词叫做名词。

（2）分类：名词通常分为专有名词和普通名词两大类。

1）专有名词一般表示具体的人、独一无二的事物以及地点或机构的专有名称。专有名词的第一个字母要大写。

e.g. Beijing、Women's Day、Yale University、Monday、Professor Smith、Thomas Edison

2）普通名词表示某类人或某类事物的名称。

e.g. fighter、country、staff、tea、happiness、information

二、名词的数

名词又可分为可数名词和不可数名词。其中，可数名词有单复数形式。

（1）可数名词的规则变化。

1）绝大多数名词的复数形式是在名词后加-s。

e.g. book – books　　　　bag – bags　　　day – days　　　map - maps

2）以字母 s、sh、ch、x 和以辅音＋o 结尾的名词后加-es。

e.g. bus – buses　　　　brush – brushes　　　　watch – watches

　　box – boxes　　　　tomato – tomatoes　　　　hero – heroes

但，photo – photos　　piano – pianos　　　　radio – radios

3）以字母 f 或 fe 结尾的名词构成复数形式时，要把 f 或 fe 改成 v，再加-es。

e.g. life – lives　　　leaf – leaves　　　shelf – shelves

但，roof – roofs　　chief – chiefs　　　proof – proofs

4）以辅音字母＋y 结尾的名词构成复数形式时，要把 y 改为 i，再加-es。

e.g. baby – babies　　　factory – factories　　　country – countries

（2）可数名词的不规则变化。

1）改变内部元音字母。

e.g. man – men　　　　woman –women　　　　foot – feet　　　　tooth – teeth

2）单、复数形式相同。

e.g. sheep, deer, means (方式、手段), series (系列), species (物种、种类), works (工厂)

3）表示"某国人"的名词的单、复数形式因习惯不同而各异。

e.g. a Chinese – two Chinese　　　a Japanese – three Japanese

an American – four Americans　　a German – five Germans

an Englishman – six Englishmen　　a Dutchman – seven Dutchmen

4）应注意复合名词的复数。

①复合名词中有主体名词，就在主体名词后加-s。

e.g. lookers-on (旁观者)　　　sisters-in-law (嫂子、弟妹等)　　　editors-in-chief (总编辑)

②复合名词中没有主体名词，就在词尾加-s。

e.g. grown-ups (成年人)　　　go-betweens (中间人)

③有些复合名词的组成部分都要变成复数形式。

e.g. men-teachers (男老师)　　women-doctors (女大夫)

5）其他形式。

e.g. a child – two children　　an ox – six oxen　　a mouse –four mice

（3）较为常见的不可数名词。

advice、baggage、bread、cash、equipment、furniture、information、knowledge、luggage、money、news、traffic、trouble、work

三、名词的格

在英语中名词有三种格：主格（作主语）、宾格（作宾语）和所有格（作定语）。其中只有所有格有形式变化。

名词的所有格表示所有关系，有以下几种形式：
（1）表示有生命的东西的名词所有格一般在名词后加's。
e.g. my sister's husband   Mr. Lin's telephone number

注意：
1）以-s 或-es 结尾的复数名词所有格只在名词后加 "'"。
e.g. the teachers' reading room   the workers' dinning-room

2）不以-s 结尾的复数名词的所有格要加's。
e.g. people's needs   women's rights

3）复合名词的所有格在后面的名词后加-s。
e.g. her son-in-law's photo   the editor-in-chief's office

4）两人共有的东西，只在后一个名词加-s；如果不是共有的，则两个名词之后都要加-s。
e.g. Jane and Helen's room   Bill's and Tom's car

5）在表示 "店铺"、"某人家" 的名词所有格后面，一般省略所修饰的名词。
e.g. the tailor's   the barber's   at my aunt's

6）有些指时间、距离、国家、城镇的无生命名词也可以加's 表示所有格。
e.g. Shanghai's industry   China's culture
     two hours' movie   ten minutes' walk

（2）表示无生命东西的名词一般与 of 构成词组，表示所有关系。
e.g. the cover of the book   the title of the song

（3）在表示所属物的名词前有冠词、数词、不定代词或指示代词时常用 "of 词组＋所有格" 的形式来表示所有关系，称为名词双重所有格。
e.g. a friend of my father's   two cousins of his

some inventions of Edison's　　　　a few classmates' of mine

Exercise 10: 将括号内的汉语译成英语。

1) My little sister has a lot of _____ (玩具).

2) Granny Li has two _____ (儿媳) and a _____ (女婿).

3) She usually goes to the cinema on _____ (星期日).

4) Please have some _____ (茶).

5) Three _____ (钥匙) have been lost by him.

Exercise 11: 选择填空。

1) Something was wrong with _____ car, but luckily they knew how to fix it.

A. Jim's and Tom's　　　　　　　B. Jim and Tom's

C. Jim's and Tom　　　　　　　　D. Jim and Tom

2) She is the only one among the _____ writers who _____ stories for children.

A. woman; writes　　　　　　　　B. women; write

C. women; writes　　　　　　　　D. woman; write

3) He gained his _____ by printing _____ of famous writers.

A. wealth; work　　　　　　　　　B. wealths; works

C. wealths; work　　　　　　　　　D. wealth; works

4) This is the first time in our _____ that we have come to Beijing.

A. life　　　　B. live　　　　　C. lives　　　　　D. lifes

5) There are four _____ and two _____ in the group.

A. Japanese; Germen　　　　　　B. Japaneses; Germen

C. Japanese; Germen　　　　　　D. Japanese; Germans

Exercise 12: 将下列词组译成英语。

1）国家的主人　　　2）学生们的作业　　　3）中国的教育

4）国际妇女节　　　5）半小时的谈话　　　6）我姨母家

7）昨天的报纸　　　8）她嫂子的两个女儿

Unit 3　Web
Communicative Samples

Conversation 1

(Sun Hai is consulting Li Ming, who majors in computer science, and knows about the Internet.)

Sun Hai: Hello, Li Ming. I wonder if you could tell me something about the Internet.

Li Ming: Sure. What exactly do you want to know?

Sun Hai: We'd better start from the beginning. What is the Internet?

Li Ming: In a word, the Internet is a network of thousands of computers connected.

Sun Hai: Nowadays people often talk about the "information superhighway". Is the Internet the same thing?

Li Ming: Not exactly.

Sun Hai: What can I find on the Internet?

Li Ming: Almost everything. You name it, and then the Internet has it.

Sun Hai: What do I need to get onto the Internet?

Li Ming: From now on, the requirements are a personal computer, a modem, a communication program, an access to a telephone line…

Sun Hai: Thank you for telling me about that.

Conversation 2

(An interviewer is talking with a hacker, Michael.)

Interviewer: Michael, when did you first get interested in the computer?

Michael:　　I was 9. It attracted me so much that I majored in computer science in college.

Interviewer: And is that when you began hacking?

Michael:　　Er…. Well, I was a freshman. I remember I broke into the college administration files one day.

Interviewer: It must have been difficult to get into it.

Michael:　　I believe it was easy. You know, the college security administrators don't do enough to protect their network's systems.

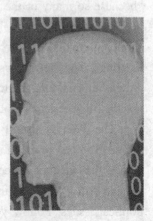

Interviewer: What did you do when you got into these systems?

Michael: I did nothing but enjoyed the satisfaction of doing it.

Interviewer: What do you plan to do after graduating?

Michael: Oh, I'd like to work as a consultant advising on security systems.

New Words and Expressions

wonder	/ˈwʌndə/	*n. v. & adj.*	惊奇
network	/ˈnetwəːk/	*n.*	网络
connect	/kəˈnekt/	*v.*	连接
requirement	/riˈkwaiəmənt/	*n.*	需求
modem	/ˈməudəm/	*n.*	调制解调器
communication	/kəˌmjuːniˈkeiʃn/	*n.*	通讯

Exercise 1: Complete the following sentences.

A: Hello, Li Ming. _____ (互联网是什么啊)?

B: _____ (简单地说), the Internet is a network of thousands of computers connected.

A: That sounds great.

B: _____ (网上都有什么啊)?

A: Almost everything. You name it, the Internet has it.

B: _____ (非常感谢你能告诉我这些).

Exercise 2: Fill in the missing letters.

w_ _der   n_tw_ _k   p_ _s_ _al   m_d_m   a_ _e_ _

h_ _k_ _   a_ _ra_ _   d_f_ _se   arr_ _t   s_ _u_ _ty

Paragraph Reading A: Welcome to the Web!

The Internet and the World Wide Web are great places to be right now. We use the term "because so many of the things you can do online are similar to the things you can do wherever people gather together—in homes, schools, libraries, shopping malls, or at family reunions or town meetings. The Net allows people to learn, shop, find crucial information, and to participate in communities, whether they're local, global, or simply virtual.

The Web is useful: You can find old friends online. You can research and book flight reservations. Check the weather. Check out your high school or college Alma Master. Find breaking news. Research political issues. Follow your stock portfolio. Place a

Copyright-Digital Vision   Business Computer Graphics

classified ad. and, of course, more and more vendors are setting up shops on the Web and selling books, CDs, computers, even cars.

The Internet is also fun. You can write to old friends. Or check out their web pages. Enjoy web-based soap operas. Laugh at online parodies and jokes. Join in a live Net Event. Chat with other Internet surfers. Pick a fake stock portfolio. Check to see if your name appears anywhere on the Web. There's a lot of fun on the web. That's one reason why it's called web "surfing".

New Words and Expressions

Internet	/'intənet/	*n.*	因特网
WWW (World Wide Web)			万维网
term	/təːm/	*n.*	学期
online	/ɔn'lain/	*n.*	联机
similar	/'similə/	*adj.*	相似的
gather	/'gæðə/	*n. & v.*	集合
reunion	/riːˈjuːnjən/	*n.*	团圆
crucial	/'kruːʃiəl/	*adj.*	至关紧要的
global	/'gləubəl/	*adj.*	球形的；全世界的
virtual	/'vəːtjuəl/	*adj.*	模拟的，虚拟的
research	/ri'səːtʃ/	*n. & v.*	研究，搜索
reservation	/ˌrezə'veiʃ ən/	*n.*	保留，预定
check	/tʃek/	*n. & v.*	核对
political	/pə'litikəl/	*adj.*	政治的
stock	/stɔk/	*n.*	股票
portfolio	/pɔːt'fəuljəu/	*n.*	投资组合,有价证券组合
vendor	/'vendɔː/	*n.*	卖主
opera	/'ɔpərə/	*n.*	歌剧
chat	/tʃæt/	*n. & v.*	聊天
surfing	/'səːfiŋ/	*n.*	网络冲浪

Exercise 3: **Select the answer that best expresses the main idea of the paragraph reading A.**

1) The main idea of the passage is that _____.

    A. The Web is useful

    B. The Internet is also fun

    C. The Internet and the World Wide Web are great places to be right now

    D. The difference between the Web and the Internet

2) According to the author, through the Web we can _____.

    A. find old friends

    B. research and book flight reservations

    C. check the weather and check out your high school or college Alma Master

    D. All of the above

3) What do we learn from paragraph 2?

    A. The Web is useful and we can do a lot of things online.

    B. Online, people can research and book flight reservations.

    C. We can set up shop on the Web.

    D. A、B and C.

4) According to the passage, why is using the web is called "surfing"?

    A. Because we can check to see whether our name appears anywhere on the Web.

    B. Because there's a lot of fun on the web.

    C. Because parodies and jokes online make us laugh.

    D. Because we can chat with other Internet surfers.

5) It can be inferred from the passage that _____.

    A. cyberspace is endless

    B. more and more businessmen are selling books, CDs, computers, even cars online

    C. many of the things we can do online are similar to the things we can do in homes, schools, libraries

    D. the Web provides us parodies and jokes

Exercise 4: Fill in the blanks with words and expressions given below. Change the form where necessary.

check out	surfing	right now	crucial	term	similar to	wherever	political
public	reunion	reservation	allow	stock	participate in	soap	

1) There is a TV show about AIDS on _____.

2) Are there any exams at the end of this _____.

3) Their house is _____ ours, but ours has a bigger garden.

4) Remember you are a Chinese _____ you go.

5) The town has its own _____ library and public gardens.

6) We hold an annual _____ of former students of the college.

7) The facts _____ of only one explanation.

8) We have succeeded in one _____ event: making this secret public.

9) Everyone in the class is expected to _____ the discussion.

10) I'd like to make a _____.

11) These are _____ rather than social matters.

12) The boss _____ the tools to the workers as they came to work.

13) The _____ slipped out of my hand.

14) If the waves are big enough, we'll go _____.

15) The store took _____ on Monday.

Exercise 5: Definitions of these words appear on the right. Put the letter of the appropriate definition next to each word.

1) _____ online   a. being in effect but not in fact

2) _____ virtual   b. the collecting of information about a subject

3) _____ surfing   c. relating to or connected to a computer

4) _____ research   d. a supply of something for use

5) _____ stock   e. ride the surf

Exercise 6: Translate the following sentences.

Five years ago, the world began to pay close attention to the Internet, but nobody ever considered online shopping.

Four years ago, the Internet was regarded only as one part of the information technology industry. Still few expected the Internet would become a new economy that would lead social development.

Three years ago, nobody imagined that all goods could be sold through the Internet. Nobody didn't believe that all commodities could be traded through e-commerce.

Paragraph Reading B: Ready, Steady, Go!

Using the Web for business or for fun is learning how to work a "web browser". If you're new to computers, it may take a while before you are completely comfortable with your browser. Don't worry. You don't have to be a computer whiz. The basics of modern computers are learning how to point and click with the mouse, learning how to scroll up and down a page of text, and learning how to use pull-down menus. There's no time limit on web surfing. Give yourself a chance to explore the browser itself while you explore the Web.

copyright digital vision   Business Connections

So, after starting to learn how your browser works, where do you go? What do you do? There's no right answer to these. The Internet doesn't have a front door. But there are lots of ways to get started. Make a bookmark to an Internet guide like Yahoo, or a search engine. Then search for web sites about one of your hobbies, such as fishing, mountain bikes, crosswords puzzles, and so on. Find web sites about your hometown. Follow links to other sites listed on the site you're visiting. Just go to find web sites. Read them, print them out. Send the URLs (the web addresses) to friends. Ask friends and co-workers for recommendations. Now you're networking. Now you're surfing the Web.

New Words and Expressions

| business | /ˈbiznis/ | n. | 商业，事情 |
| browser | /brauzə/ | n. | 浏览器 |

comfortable	/ˈkʌmfətəbl/	*adj.*	舒适的
whiz	/hwiz/	*n. & v.*	能手；善于…的人
click	/klik/	*n. & v.*	突击
scroll	/skrəul/	*n. & v.*	卷轴，滚屏；滚动
menu	/ˈmenju:/	*n.*	菜单
limit	/ˈlimit/	*n. & v.*	限制
explore	/iksˈplɔ:/	*v.*	探险
bookmark	/ˈbukmɑ:k/	*n.*	书签
guide	/gaɪd/	*n. & v.*	向导，引导
crossword	/ˈkrɔswə:d/	*n.*	纵横字谜
puzzle	/ˈpʌzl/	*n. & v.*	迷惑
link	/liŋk/	*n. & v.*	连接
address	/əˈdres/	*n.*	地址
recommendation	/ˌrekəmenˈdeiʃən/	*n.*	推荐

Exercise 7: Select the answer that best expresses the main idea of the paragraph reading B.

1) The topic of paragraph 1 is that _____.

　　A. surfing on web is not limited by time

　　B. exploring the browser itself

　　C. how to use pull-down menus

　　D. how to use a "web browser" when we use the Web for business or for fun

2) In line 1, the word "browser" refers to _____.

　　A. a modem

　　B. a machine that helps people to search information on line

　　C. a mouse

　　D. a screen

3) We can find the web sites through _____.

　　A. making a bookmark to an Internet guide

　　B. searching for web sites about your hobby

　　C. finding web sites about your hometown

　　D. all of the above

4) There are lots of ways to get starting the Internet except _____.

　　A. clicking with the mouse

　　B. making a tag to a search engine

　　C. making a bookmark to an Internet guide like Yahoo

　　D. finding web sites

5) According to the first Paragraph, it can be inferred that _____.

　　A. there's no limitation on web surfing　　B. the Internet doesn't have a front door

　　C. learning how to work a "web browser"　　D. it's useful to make bookmarks

Exercise 8: Fill in the blanks with words and expressions given below. Change the form where necessary.

mountain	so on	guide	point	click	engine	mouse	chance	explore
print out	Internet	bookmark	search for		crossword			comfortable

1) It's only human nature to want a _____ life.

2) I don't see the _____ of her last remark.

3) That's the _____ of the switch.

4) The cat made a spring at the _____.

5) I never miss a _____ of playing football.

6) The experts are _____ every part of the island.

7) _____ plays a very important role in modern life.

8) Another time he was seen using a check for $1500 as a _____ . Then he lost the book!

9) He _____ the man through the streets to the railway station.

10) He lost one of the pieces of his model _____.

11) The company is casting its net wide in its _____ a new sales director.

12) The _____ tops are covered with snow.

13) I finished the _____ (all) by myself.

14) He talked about how much we owed to our parents, our duty to our country and _____.

15) You may use an online printer to _____ the data.

Exercise 9: Definitions of these words appear on the right. Put the letter of the appropriate definition next to each word.

1) _____ scroll   a. confuse the understanding of

2) _____ puzzle   b. the act of recommending

3) _____ recommendation   c. a roll of paper or animal skin

4) _____ explore   d. a point beyond which a person or thing cannot go

5) _____ limit   e. search through

Grammar Focus: Articles 冠词

一、冠词的定义和分类

（1）定义：冠词是一种虚词，没有词义，没有数和格的变化，不能单独使用，只能帮助名词或起名词的作用的其他词类，说明其意义。

（2）分类：冠词分为不定冠词 a、an 和定冠词 the 两种。

二、不定冠词 a、an 的一般用法

（1）表示"一"或"一个"。

e.g. a book，a chair，an apple，an hour，a university

（2）泛指，表示某类人或东西中的一个。

There is a new book on the desk.

Lend me a novel, will you?

（3）概括人或事物的整体，表示一类。

e.g. A bike is very useful in the countryside.

　　A horse has four legs.

（4）在表示时间、速度、价格等意义的名词之前，表示"每一"。

e.g. She drinks milk three times a day.

　　We have an English dictation once a week.

（5）用于专有、物质、抽象名词前，表示"某一位"、"一个"、"某种"之含义。

e.g. A Mr. Smith is waiting for you.

　　He has a great love for art.

（6）疾病名称前一般不用冠词，但常见病名称前，要加不定冠词。

e.g. cold，cough，fever，temperature，headache，ache，pain

（7）用于由动词转化成的名词前。

e.g. break，drive，kick，look，rest，sleep，smoke，wash，weep

（8）用于固定搭配。

e.g. a bit of，a few，a little，a great deal of，a lot of

　　have a good time，have a word with，go out for a walk

　　once upon a time，many a time，a long time，a short time

　　as a result，as a whole，at a loss，at a time

　　in a hurry，in a moment，in a word

三、定冠词 the 的一般用法

（1）在表示"前面已说过的人或事物"的名词之前。

e.g. I bought a dictionary yesterday. The dictionary is now on the bookshelf.

（2）在表示"说话人与听话人都知道的共同所指的事物"的名词之前。

e.g. Shut the door, please.

　　Please look at the blackboard.

（3）给予表示一般意义的名词以明确的、限定的或特指的意义。

e.g. The butter I bought is not cheap.

I like the music composed by that man.

（4）在表示独一无二的事物的名词之前。

e.g. the sun，the sky，the moon，the earth，the world，the Great wall

（5）用于姓氏的复数名词之前，表示"一家人"。

e.g. The Greens have moved to the new house.

The Browns are at home today.

（6）在表示乐器名称的名词之前。

e.g. He likes playing the piano / the violin / the guitar.

（7）在形容词和副词最高级之前，但副词最高级前的 the 可省略。

e.g. Winter is the coldest season of the year.

Who does the homework (the) most carefully in your class?

（8）在序数词之前。

e.g. He is always the last one to come and the first one to leave.

（9）在方向名词和表示时间的词组或习惯用语之前。

e.g. in the east，on the right，in the end，in the morning，in the daytime

（10）代替所有格代词，指已提到过的人身体的某一部分或衣服的一部分。

e.g. He angrily hit Mr. Smith in the face.

The brave old woman seized a thief by the collar.

（11）在某些形容词之前，表示一类人。

e.g. the young，the old，the blind，the wounded，the progressive

（12）在表示单位的名词之前。

e.g. I have hired the car by the hour.

Eggs are sold by the dozen.

（13）在由 of 词组修饰的名词之前。

e.g. Do you still remember the name of the city?

Most of the students think English is important and useful.

（14）用于固定搭配。

e.g. at the moment，at the most，by the way，for the time being

in the distance，in the end，in the long run，on average
on the contrary，on the whole

四、不用冠词的场合

（1）复数可数名词或不可数名词泛指时。

e.g. Life mainly depends on water.

I like flowers.

（2）在称呼、职务名称之前。

e.g. Clinton is president of the United States.

Mr. Brown is my father's old friend.

（3）在表示三餐的名词之前。

e.g. I like rice for supper.

He often goes to school without breakfast.

（4）在表示球类和游戏名称的名词之前。

e.g. play basketball / volleyball / football / chess / cards

（5）在表示星期、月份、季节等时间的名词之前。

e.g. We have classes from Monday to Friday.

March is the third month of a year.

Do you like skating in winter?

（6）在由 by 引导的表示运输、输送工具的名词之前。

e.g. by air，by bicycle，by bus，by car，by land，by sea，by radio，by telephone，by telex，by post，by mail

但，这些名词前如果用了其他介词，则需加冠词 the。

e.g. They are talking on the phone.

（7）在某些习惯用语中的名词之前，以具体名词表示抽象概念。

e.g. School begins in September.

The thief was thrown into prison.

Exercise 10: 用适当的冠词填空。

1) It's raining now. Take _____ raincoat with you. _____ raincoat is in my bag.

2) _____ sun rises in _____ east and sets in _____ west.

3) His mother is _____ English teacher. She teaches in _____ primary school.

4) She is _____ youngest student in our class.

5) We have three meals _____ day. We have breakfast at seven in _____ morning every day.

Exercise 11: 选择填空。

1) She is ill and now in _____ hospital. I'm going to _____ hospital to see her.

    A. the; a   B. a; the   C. /; a   D. /; the

2) Lesson Three is _____ most difficult lesson, but it isn't _____ most difficult lesson in Book Two.

    A. a; a   B. a; the   C. the; the   D. the; a

3) _____ word came that he had come back.

    A. The   B. /   C. A   D. An

4) ——How did you pay the workers?

    ——As a rule, they were paid _____ .

    A. by the hour   B. by an hour   C. by a hour   D. by hours

5) One way to understand thousands of new words is to gain _____ good knowledge of basic word formation.

    A. /   B. the   C. a   D. one

6) I don't like talking on _____ telephone; I prefer writing _____ letters.

    A. a; the   B. the; /   C. the; the   D. a; /

7) Our teacher often says to us, "Be _____ honest boy today and _____ useful man tomorrow".

    A. an; a   B. a; a   C. a; an   D. an; an

8) None but _____ were respected.

    A. brave   B. a brave   C. braves   D. the brave

9) The boy was not hit in _____ face, but on _____ head.

    A. his; his   B. the; the   C. his; the   D. the; his

10) We have begun to learn _____ Japanese language.

    A. a   B. /   C. the   D. an

Unit 4　Climate & Weather
Communicative Samples

Conversation 1

(Kelly and McKee are talking about the weather.)

Kelly:　Lovely day, isn't it?

McKee: Yes, it is. The sunshine, the fresh air, everything is so wonderful.

Kelly:　But do you know there was a terrible rainstorm last night. It rained cats and dogs!

McKee: Lucky for me that it come after I had enjoyed a lovely day.

Kelly:　Absolutely. The weather forecast says that it's going to be fair and sunny today.

McKee: I hope it will stay fine. Actually there's no wind.

Kelly:　You're absolutely right. You have come in the best season, too.

McKee: That's great. I like sunshine.

Kelly:　What's the weather like in your hometown, McKee?

McKee: It's not so nice. Sometimes it even rains for two or three days in succession.

Kelly:　That's awful. I hope you'll enjoy your stay here and the nice weather as well.

McKee: I certainly will. Thank you.

Conversation 2

(Karen and Rose are talking about the weather.)

Karen: What a lovely day! Don't you think so?

Rose:　Yeah. It's calm. I like the peace.

Karen: Look, there are some clouds.

Rose:　That's the sign of wind.

Karen: Oh, really, I thought it was a sign of rain.

Rose:　This summer is too rainy for me.

Karen: We didn't see the sun for very long.

Rose:　Especially, the farmers suffered a lot from the heavy rain.

Karen: Look at the thick clouds. I think it's going to rain again.

Karen: Let's go home now.

Rose:　Ok, I hope it will clear up soon.

New Words and Expressions

sunshine	/ˈsʌnʃain/	n.	阳光
rainstorm	/reinˈstɔːm/	n.	暴风雨
weather	/ˈweðə/	n. v. & adj.	天气
forecast	/ˈfɔːkɑːst/	n. & v.	预报
sunny	/ˈsʌni/	adj.	阳光充足的
succession	/səkˈseʃən/	n.	连续

Exercise 1: Complete the following sentences.

A: Hi, Lucy. Nice and bright this morning.

B: _____ (是呀，比昨天好多了).

A: The wind will pick up later.

B: _____ (只要不下雨就行).

A: Yes. If the weather is fine, we are planning go to the Great Wall.

B: _____ (太好了).

Exercise 2: Fill in the missing letters.

w_ _ther   ra_ _s_ _rm   fr_ _h   br_ _ze   sh_ _ing

c_lm   clo_d   r_ _ny   p_ _ce   s_ff_ _

Paragraph Reading A: How to Measure Distance in California

People in California often measure distance in driving time, not in miles. They say, "San Francisco is eight hours from Los Angeles." It takes two and a half hours to get to Palm Springs from Los Angeles. "Arrowhead is three hours from Los Angeles."

Short distances separate extremes in California's climate. You can swim in the ocean at one of the beach cities in the morning. From the beach, you can drive about two hours and eat lunch at a desert resort. Then you can drive to the mountains and ski in the afternoon.

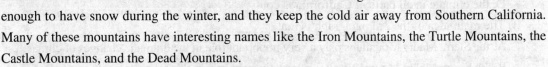

The Sierra Madre Mountains cause the dramatic changes of climate in short distances. Some of these mountains are high enough to have snow during the winter, and they keep the cold air away from Southern California. Many of these mountains have interesting names like the Iron Mountains, the Turtle Mountains, the Castle Mountains, and the Dead Mountains.

The ocean wind comes in and keeps the coastline warm. Warm air from the ocean can't get over the mountains, so it stops at the desert. The sun shines on the desert sand. The mountains also keep the rain away, so the desert is hot and dry.

The beautiful mountains, desert, and beach areas attract many people. The easiest way to get to these places is by car, so everyone drives. As long as people drive to these places, they will continue to measure the distance in hours, not in miles.

New Words and Expressions

California	/ˌkæliˈfɔːnjə/	n.	加利福尼亚
measure	/ˈmeʒə/	n. & v.	测量
San Francisco		n.	旧金山
Los Angeles		n.	洛杉矶
palm	/pɑːm/	n.	棕榈；手掌
spring	/spriŋ/	n. & v.	春天；温泉
separate	/ˈsepəreit/	adj. & v.	分开的
extreme	/iksˈtriːm/	n. & adj.	极端，极端的
climate	/ˈklaimit/	n.	气候
beach	/ˈbiːtʃ/	n.	海滩
desert	/diˈzəːt/	n.	沙漠
resort	/riˈzɔːt/	n.	旅游胜地，度假胜地
dramatic	/drəˈmætik/	adj.	戏剧性的
coastline	/ˈkəustlain/	n.	海岸线
sand	/sænd/	n.	沙
attract	/əˈtrækt/	v.	吸引

Exercise 3:   Select the answer that best expresses the main idea of the paragraph reading A.

1) The main idea of this selection is _____.

    A. people in California drive all the time

    B. people in California drive to work

    C. people in California measure distance in driving time

    D. people in California measure distance in miles

2) The main idea of the 2nd paragraph is _____.

    A. the climate in all parts of California is the same

    B. the climate in all parts of California is hot

    C. the climate in all parts of California is completely different

    D. the climate in all parts of California is cold

3) The main idea of the 3rd paragraph is that _____.

    A. the Sierra Madre Mountains play a very important role in the dramatic changes of climate

    B. the Sierra Madre Mountains play an unimportant role in the dramatic changes of climate

    C. the Atlantic Ocean plays a very important role in the dramatic changes of climate

    D. the desert plays a very important role in the dramatic changes of climate

4) The word "extremes" in the sentence "Short distances separate extremes in California's climate" means _____.

    A. quality that is as widely different as possible

    B. quality that is as good as possible

    C. differences

    D. similarities

5) The main idea of the 4th paragraph is _____.

    A. why the desert is hot and dry   B. where the desert is located

    C. how people get to the desert   D. how the desert came into being

Exercise 4: Fill in the blanks with words and expressions given below. Change the form where necessary.

decide	as long as	distance	coastline	separate	extreme	climate
beach	drive to attract	dramatic	keep away	get over	measure	enough

1) The government has promised to take _____ to help the unemployed.

2) We can see the mountain from the _____.

3) The war _____ many families.

4) The capital is in the _____ south of the country.

5) North America has the world's best _____ for wild grapes.

6) They walked along the _____ talking and laughing.

7) The writer _____ to live in the Sahara Desert for some time.

8) How long does it take him to _____ work?

9) After a _____ pause, the lawyer finished her speech.

10) Nobody can entirely _____ from this competitive world.

11) As evening came the _____ faded into darkness.

12) I can't _____ how much your children have grown.

13) Do you have _____ time to finish the paper?

14) The flower show _____ large crowds this year.

15) _____ you drive carefully, you will be very safe.

Exercise 5: Definitions of these words appear on the right. Put the letter of the appropriate definition next to each word.

1) _____ measure   a. the space or amount of space between two points, lines, surfaces, or objects

2) _____ distance   b. the outline or shape of a coast

3) _____ coastline   c. draw by appealing to interest or feeling

4) _____ separate   d. the act or process of measuring

5) _____ attract   e. set or keep apart

Exercise 6: Translate the following sentences.

Thousands of years ago people found out that days were longer in summer than in winter, and nights were shorter. They determined through the observation that the day was shortest in the Northern Hemisphere on the 22nd of December, after which it gradually grew longer until the 21st of June when the day was the longest in the year and the night was the shortest.

Paragraph Reading B: Hurricane

Lowell Genzlinger is a pilot who looks for a hurricane. He can let people know when a hurricane might be coming. A hurricane is a huge storm with a big eye. There is a strong wind around this eye. But in the eye of a hurricane, the air is quiet.

A hurricane is eye strong. The strong wind of a hurricane can snap a tree in two or turn over a big boat. There may be a flood with a hurricane. Last summer, Lowell saw a hurricane flood a city in just one hour.

Tonight, pictures from satellites in the sky show some strange clouds over the ocean. Could they be a hurricane? Lowell is asked to pilot his plane through the clouds. Firstly, Lowell can see the stars in the sky. Then, slowly, black clouds move around his plane. The wind is roaring now. Lowell must get to the eye of this hurricane. He calls to land by radio. "I can't fly in a line through this storm. The wind is too strong and I have to fly left." All around Lowell's plane, the storm is roaring with lightning and thunder. The wind and rain rock the plane.

Then the wind and the rain stop. All around his plane, Lowell can see a line of clouds where lightning and thunder are. But where he is now, the air is quiet. He is in the eye of the Hurricane!

New Words and Expressions

pilot	/ˈpailət/	n. & v.	飞行员，驾驶
hurricane	/ˈhʌrikən/	n.	飓风
huge	/hjuːdʒ/	adj.	巨大的
snap	/snæp/	v.	（使）断裂，绷断
flood	/flʌd/	n. & v.	洪水，淹没
satellite	/ˈsætəlait/	n.	人造卫星
roar	/rɔː/	n. & v.	吼叫，咆哮
thunder	/ˈθʌndə/	n. & v.	雷，打雷

Exercise 7: Select the answer that best expresses the main idea of the paragraph reading B.

1) Lowell is a pilot who can fly _____.

    A. to the stars   B. through a hurricane

    C. over the mountains   D. over the ocean

2) Lowell must fly his plane _____.

    A. to find out if the weather is good   B. to find out where a big city is

    C. to find out when it rains   D. to find out what the clouds are

3) A hurricane can _____.

    A. break a tree   B. turn over boats at sea

    C. flood a city   D. all of the above

4) The "eye" of a hurricane is _____.

    A. the cloudless center of a hurricane where there is just quiet air

    B. the lightning in the middle of the hurricane

    C. the cloudy center of a storm where there is just quiet air

    D. the thunder over the clouds

5) When Lowell gets to the eye of the hurricane, _____.

    A. he is in danger   B. he can see nothing

    C. he is safe   D. the lightning will hit him

Exercise 8: Fill in the blanks with words and expressions given below. Change the form where necessary.

| through | look for | satellite | line | quiet | snap | lightning | turn …over |
| flood | ask to | pilot | move around | | roar | thunder | in the sky |

1) He turned on the torch to _____ his keys.

2) When he _____ down, I began to tell him the truth.

3) The fish _____ at the bait.

4) He _____ the business _____ to his daughter.

5) Japanese cars have _____ the American market.

6) Television stations around the world are linked by _____.

7) John was _____ deliver a speech on the graduation.

8) Mark used to be a _____ on the Mississippi River.

9) A cloud is a mass of vapor _____.

10) These stars appear to _____ the North Star.

11) It's a poor teacher who can only control the class by _____ at the pupils.

12) The river flows _____ the city from east to west.

13) There were many flashes of _____ during the storm.

14) We could hear the _____ of distant guns.

15) Hang the clothes on the _____.

Exercise 9: Definitions of these words appear on the right. Put the letter of the appropriate definition next to each word.

1) _____ hurricane   a. a heavenly body orbiting another of larger size

2) _____ satellite   b. to make a sudden closing of the jaws

3) _____ thunder   c. a cyclone formed in the tropics with winds

4) ＿＿＿＿＿ snap 　　　　d. to utter a long full loud sound
5) ＿＿＿＿＿ roar 　　　　e. the loud sound that follows a flash of lightning

Grammar Focus: Pronouns 代词（一）

一、代词的定义和种类
代词是为了避免重复而用来代替名词的词。

英语中的代词共有 9 种：人称代词、物主代词、反身代词、相互代词、指示代词、疑问代词、关系代词、连接代词和不定代词。

大多数代词具有名词和形容词的作用。

二、人称代词
人称代词有人称、性、数、格之分。英语中主要有下面这些人称代词：

人称 ＼ 数格	单　　数		复　　数	
	主格	宾格	主格	宾格
第一人称	I	me	we	us
第二人称	you	you	you	you
第三人称	he	him	they	them
	she	her		
	it	it		

（1）人称代词的主格在句中作主语。
e.g. They are playing football on the playground.
　　　You, she and I all enjoy pop music.
（注意：几个人称代词同时作主语时，you 在最前，I、we 在最后。）
The moon is shining brightly, she is like a round silvery plate.
（注意：表示国家、船只、大地、月亮等的名词常用 she 代替。）

（2）人称代词的宾格在句中作动词宾语或介词宾语。
e.g. Our English teacher taught us an English song.
　　　His parents are looking for him.

（3）要注意人称代词 it 的特殊用法。
e.g. Look at that poor little child, it has just fallen down.
　　　It is necessary to buy that dictionary.
　　　I consider it important to ask him for advice.
　　　It is five o'clock.

It is fine today.

It is the bicycle that I bought yesterday.

三、物主代词

表示所有关系的代词叫物主代词，可分为形容词性物主代词和名词性物主代词两大类。

人 称	形 容 词 性		名 词 性	
	单数	复数	单数	复数
第一人称	my	our	mine	ours
第二人称	your	your	yours	yours
第三人称	his	their	his	theirs
	her	their		

（1）形容词性物主代词用作定语。

e.g. my childhood，our task，his view，her students，their difficulties

注意，形容词性物主代词除了作定语之外，还可放在动名词短语之前，作短语的逻辑主语。

e.g. Do you mind my opening the door?

His coming made us very happy.

We can't believe her breaking the law.

（2）名词性物主代词用作主语、表语和宾语。

e.g. His brother is a doctor, mine is a manager.

—Whose computer is it?   —It is mine.

You may use my bike, and I may use hers.

注意，"of + 名词性物主代词"可用作定语。

e.g. Wang Ling is an old classmate of ours.

The baby of hers is so lovely!

四、反身代词

表示"我自己"、"你自己"、"他自己"、"我们自己"、"你们自己"、"他们自己"的代词称为反身代词。

数 人称	单 数	复 数
第一人称	myself	ourselves
第二人称	yourself	yourselves
第三人称	himself, herself, itself	themselves

（1）用作宾语时，反身代词含有"自己"的意思，既是动作的执行者，又是动作的承受者。

e.g. He can look after himself.

　　They enjoyed themselves at Disneyland.

（2）反身代词也可以在句中作名词、代词的同位语，起强调作用。表示"亲自、本人"的意思，置于名词、代词的后面或句末。

e.g. I myself took Mary to the airport.

　　I will tell John himself what you want.

　　She opened the door herself.

（3）反身代词还可以构成某些惯用语。

e.g. by oneself 单独、独自地　　　between oneself 私下地；保密地

　　of oneself 自动地　　　　　　for oneself 独立地；亲自地

五、指示代词

表示"这个"、"那个"、"这些"、"那些"、"如此的"、"同样的"等指示概念的代词称为指示代词。

指示代词有：this、that、these、those、such、the same 等。

（1）指示代词在句中作主语、表语、宾语或定语。

e.g. That is a good idea.

　　What I want is this.

　　He didn't like that.

　　These pictures are very beautiful.

（2）this 和 these 常指后面要讲到的事物，有启下的作用；而 that 和 those 常指前面将到过事物，有承上的作用。

e.g. What I want to tell you is this: The meeting is put off till Friday.

　　He had a bad cold. That is why he didn't attend the meeting.

（3）such 一般在句中作定语和主语。such 表示"这样一个…"常用于结构"such…as…"中。

e.g. Foreign friends often visit such fine cities as Beijing and Xi'an.

注意：当 such 作定语时，如果所修饰的名词前有不定冠词，则将不定冠词放在 such 之后。

e.g. We have never seen such a tall building.

（4）same 可作定语、表语、主语、宾语，该词前必须加 the。

e.g. She went to swim and I'll do the same.

Exercise 10: 选择填空。

1) Tom felt that he knew everybody's business better than they knew it _____.

　A. themselves　　　B. oneself　　　C. itself　　　D. himself

2) —Is your camera like Bill's and Tom's?

　—No, but it's almost the same as _____.

　A. her　　　B. yours　　　C. them　　　D. their

3) China will always do what _____ has promised to do.

　A. that　　　B. we　　　C. she　　　D. they

4) John's mother kept telling him that he should work harder, but _____ didn't help.

　A. he　　　B. which　　　C. she　　　D. it

5) _____ was because of her cruelty that we all hated her.

　A. It　　　B. What　　　C. That　　　D. Such

6) Jane is not quite _____ these days, so I advise you to let her alone.

　A. her　　　B. hers　　　C. herself　　　D. none

7) What I want to tell you is _____: the meeting was put off till Saturday.

　A. it　　　B. this　　　C. that　　　D. its

8) He has broken his leg. _____ is why he was absent from work.

　A. This　　　B. It　　　C. That　　　D. There

9) As I know, there is _____ car in this neighborhood.

　A. no a　　　B. no such　　　C. not such　　　D. no such a

10) We must remember that _____ fashion is not the most important thing in _____ life.

　A. /; the　　　B. /; /　　　C. the; /　　　D. the; the

Exercise 11: 将下列句子译成英语。

1）我的书在哪儿？你的书不在这儿，这是我的。

2）这些是我们的杂志，他们的在书架上。

3）这些高大的树是十年前校长亲自种的。

4）她经常帮助我学数学，而我经常教她讲英语。

5）我们的老师经常给我们讲一些我们国家的历史

Unit 5   Culture

Communicative Samples

Conversation 1

(Jackson is a foreign student in U.S.)

Lucy: Hi, Jackson. Thanksgiving Day is round the corner.

Jackson: Yes, that's right. Time flies.

Lucy: I am thinking of a Thanksgiving feast. I'd like to invite you.

Jackson: Great! Is there a special story behind this holiday?

Lucy: Yeah. The early settlers had a good harvest. They believed God gave them the harvest.

Jackson: So they wanted to show thanks to God?

Lucy: You got it.

Jackson: What do you do on Thanksgiving Day? What should I do?

Lucy: You don't have to do anything, just turn up. We are going to prepare a big feast.

Jackson: What is the main food?

Lucy: Turkey, it is a big bird like a chicken, but much bigger than chicken.

Jackson: It must be delicious.

Lucy: Of course.

Conversation 2

(A Chinese student, Li Li and her American friend are talking about the restaurant dos and don'ts with each other.)

Li Li: We have to pay much attention to some dos and don'ts in a Western restaurant.

Linda: Exactly. When you want to eat at a Western restaurant, you should first consider making a reservation.

Li Li: If not, then what will happen?

Linda: You may risk having to wait for a long time for a table.

Li Li: Anything else?

Linda: When eating, the Japanese and some Chinese are in the habit of slurping their food.

Li Li: Then how do Westerners respond to the manner?

Linda: They find eating soup in this way most unpleasant.

Li Li: What about tipping?

Linda: When it comes to tipping, they just leave some money on the table. The amount is up to you, but it's usually 15 to 20 percent of the check.

Li Li: I see.

New Words and Expressions

feast	/fiːst/	n.	盛宴
settler	/'setlə/	n.	移民者
prepare	/pri'pɛə/	v.	准备
harvest	/'hɑːvist/	n. & v.	收获
turkey	/'təːki/	n.	火鸡
pumpkin	/'pʌmpkin/	n.	南瓜
restaurant	/'restərːŋ/	n.	餐馆
attention	/ə'tenʃən/	n.	注意
slurp	/sləːp/	n.	啧啧吃的声音
tip	/tip/	n. & v.	小费；给小费
percent	/pə'sent/	n.	百分比

Exercise 1: Complete the following sentences.

A: _____ (嗨，李明)！

B: Hi, Jackson.

A: _____ (圣诞节马上就要到了).

B: Really?

A: _____ (当然是了).

B: Time flies.

Exercise 2: Fill in the missing letters.

f _ _eign   corn_ _   f _ _st   s _ _cial   har _ _st

de _ _ci _ _s   att _ _tion   c _ _sid _ _   sl _ _p   s _ _p

Paragraph Reading A: Father's Day

The idea of a special day to honour mothers was first put forward in America in 1907. Two years later a woman, Mrs. John Bruce Dodd, in the state of Washington proposed a similar day to honour the head of the family – the father. Her mother died when she was very young, and she was brought up by her father. She loved her father very much.

In response to Mrs. Dodd's idea that same year—1909, the state governor of Washington

officially proclaimed the third Sunday in June Father's Day. The idea was officially approved by President Woodrow Wilson in 1961. In 1924, President Calvin Coolidge recommended national observance of the occasion " to establish more intimate relations between fathers and their children, and to impress upon fathers the full measure of their obligations," The red or white rose is recognized as the official Fathers' Day flower.

Father's Day seems to be much less important an occasion than the Mother's Day. Not many of the children offer their fathers some presents. But the American fathers still think they are much better fated than the fathers of many other countries, who don't even have a day named for their sake.

New Words and Expressions

honour	/'ɔnə/	n. & v.	荣誉，尊敬
propose	/prə'pəuz/	v.	建议
response	/ris'pɔns/	n.	回答，回应
official	/ə'fiʃəl/	n. & adj.	官员，官方的
proclaim	/prə'kleim/	v.	宣布，声明
approve	/ə'pru:v/	v.	批准
president	/'prezidənt/	n.	总统，校长
recommend	/rekə'mend/	v.	推荐
national	/'næʃənəl/	adj.	国家的
observance	/əb'zə:vəns/	n.	遵守
occasion	/ə'keiʒən/	n.	场合，时机
establish	/is'tæbliʃ/	v.	建立
intimate	/'intimit/	adj.	亲密的
relation	/ri'leiʃən/	n.	关系
obligation	/,ɔbli'geiʃən/	n.	义务
recognize	/'rekəgnaiz/	v.	承认，认为

Exercise 3:　Select the answer that best expresses the main idea of the paragraph reading A.

1) When was the idea of Father's Day first put forward?

A. 1907　　　　　　B. 1908　　　　　　C. 1909　　　　　　D. 1910

2) Who responded to Mrs. Dodd's idea that a similar day to honor the father should be established?

A. Mrs. Dodd　　　　　　　　　　　　　B. Calvin Coolidge

C. Washington　　　　　　　　　　　　　D. Woodrow Wilson

3) The key point of the paragraph 3 is that _____.

    A. fathers in American cannot accept gifts

    B. Mother's Day is more important than Father's Day in America

    C. American fathers are superior to fathers in other countries'

    D. American fathers are good

4) According to the passage, all of the following are true except _____.

    A. the red or white rose is recognized as the official Fathers' Day flower

    B. no children offer their fathers some presents

    C. Father's Day seems to be much less important an occasion than the Mother's Day

    D. the idea of a special day to honor mothers was first put forward in America in 1907

5) What is implied in the passage?

    A. American fathers aren't much better fated than the fathers in many other countries.

    B. There is no formal Father's Day in other countries.

    C. Father's Day seems to be much more important than the Mother's Day.

    D. Many of the children offer their fathers some presents.

Exercise 4: Fill in the blanks with words and expressions given below. Change the form where necessary.

relation	in response to	special	occasion	recommend	propose	honour	bring up
governor	proclaim	approve	establish	intimate	recognize	put forward	

  1) Take _____ care tonight because the road is icy.

  2) These foreigners have _____ a proposal for a joint venture.

  3) He _____ that a change should be made.

  4) I promise I'll pay you back, on my _____.

  5) We need to _____ more tanks.

  6) Millions of people gave freely _____ the appeal.

  7) He was elected _____ of the state of California.

  8) His accent _____ that he was an American.

  9) You can join in the class if you parents _____.

  10) Our company was _____ in 1994.

  11) I wouldn't _____ you to go there alone.

  12) He should listen to his _____ feelings.

  13) Our two countries have had trade _____ for ten years.

  14) Can you _____ her from this picture?

  15) There was no _____ to be so rude.

Exercise 5: Definitions of these words appear on the right. Put the letter of the appropriate definition next to each word.

  1) _____ response   a. think well of

  2) _____ recommend   b. an act or instance of replying

3) _____ obligation   c. an act of making oneself responsible for doing something

4) _____ approve   d. make a statement in praise of

5) _____ proclaim   e. announce publicly

Exercise 6: Translate the following sentences.

Christmas Day, December 25, is perhaps the happiest day of the year for most English children. They have the pleasure to give presents to each other.

English children, always hang a stocking at the end of the bed on Christmas Eve. In the morning they play with the new toys. At lunch, there is a Christmas cake. Usually their parents will put a coin or two inside it and part of the fun is to see who finds it.

Paragraph Reading B: Holidays & Vacation

Holidays in the United States usually occur at least once a month. Most months have a national holiday that has been arranged on Monday. The holidays are celebrated on Monday so that the workers may have 3-day weekends, that is, Saturday, Sunday and Monday in order to rest or travel or do things with their families. Major holidays in the Untied States include New Year's Day, Christmas Day and Thanksgiving Day, when we remember the first settlers of the United States, called Thanksgiving Day. In these holidays most businesses close and the workers stay at home and celebrate with their families.

Vacation can be from 2 weeks a year to 4 weeks a year. This usually depends on how long you've been working for a company, what type of position you have, whether you have a very high and important position and whether you can find someone to replace you. In this case, you might take a few days at a time rather than take one month all at once. Usually the more time you spend working for a company, the more time you may get for a vacation.

New Words and Expressions

holiday	/ˈhɔlədi/	n.	假日
occur	/əˈkəː/	v.	发生
arrange	/əˈreindʒ/	v.	安排
celebrate	/ˈselibreit/	v.	庆祝
include	/inˈkluːd/	v.	包含
vacation	/vəˈkeiʃən/	n. & v.	假期

depend	/di'pend/	v.	依靠
type	/taip/	n. & v.	类型，打字
position	/pə'ziʃən/	n. & v.	位置，安置

Exercise 7: Select the answer that best expresses the main idea of the paragraph reading B.

1) The government of the U.S makes it a rule for workers to have _____ weekends.

   A. 5-day   B. 2-day   C. 3-day   D. 4-day

2) Workers in the U.S sometimes work from _____.

   A. Monday to Saturday   B. Saturday to Monday

   C. Thursday to Friday   D. Tuesday to Friday

3) Which of the following is WRONG according to this passage?

   A. Only a few shops remain open on New Year's Day.

   B. Most of the workers needn't work on Christmas Day.

   C. In the United States, there's only one holiday in a month.

   D. All the workers have a half-month vacation a year at least.

4) The reason why someone has to divide his vacation into several parts is that _____.

   A. he doesn't want to take a long vacation

   B. he hasn't a high position

   C. he plays an important role in his work

   D. he hasn't been working for his company for a long time

5) Which is the best title for this passage?

   A. Holiday in the United States.

   B. Vacation in the United States.

   C. How the Workers Spend Their Holidays.

   D. Something About the Holidays and Vacation in the U.S..

Exercise 8: Fill in the blanks with words and expressions given below. Change the form where necessary.

include	occur	vacation	at least	position	national	celebrate	major	
settler	business	depend on	replace	rather than	travel	arrange		

1) That plane crash _____ only minutes after take-off.

2) We should brush our teeth _____ twice a day.

3) The _____ news comes after the international news.

4) I _____ the flowers in the vase as soon as I came back home.

5) They _____ his success by opening a bottle of wine.

6) We have encountered _____ problems.

7) He met many interesting people in his _____ .

8) My job doesn't _____ making coffee for the boss!

9) One of his friends was an early _____ in America.

10) They've done some _____ together.

11) Children _____ their parents for food and clothing.

12) The runners got into _____ on the starting line.

13) We've _____ the old adding machine with a computer.

14) She is a career woman _____ a housewife.

15) Where did you pass the _____?

Exercise 9: Definitions of these words appear on the right. Put the letter of the appropriate definition next to each word.

1) _____ celebrate   a. a person who settles in a new region

2) _____ settler   b. the point or area occupied by something

3) _____ occur   c. come into existence

4) _____ position   d. make plans for

5) _____ arrange   e. perform publicly and according to certain rules

Grammar Focus: Pronoun 代词（二）

六、疑问代词

疑问代词 what、which、who、whom、whose 可用来构成特殊疑问句，在句中可作主语、宾语、定语和表语。

e.g. Who is standing there?

  What are you doing here?

  Whose chair is this?

  This is what he said.

七、不定代词

不明确指代某个特定名词的代词称为不定代词。常见的不定代词有：some、any、somebody、anybody、someone、anyone、something、anything、no、all、everybody、nobody、everyone、no one、everything、nothing、either、neither、one、none、both、each、another、other、others、few、a few、many、much、little、a little 等。

不定代词具有名词和形容词的性质，并有可数和不可数之分，在句中可以作主语、表语、宾语、同位语、定语及状语等。

（1）不定代词作主语时，要明确该词究竟是单数还是复数，以确定它和谓语动词在人称和数的一致关系。

e.g. Both of us are not teachers.

  Neither of us is teacher.

  None of the students are here.

  None of the money is mine.

  Nothing can stop me doing that.

All were present at the party.

All goes well.

（2）不定代词作定语时，有的修饰可数名词，如 many、few；有的修饰不可数名词，如 much、little；有的既可修饰可数名词，也可修饰不可数名词，如 some、any。

e.g. I have some water but I have not any tea.

In our library there are many books but few magazines.

Please give me another ten minutes.

There are trees on either side of the road.

Every student in our class has a Chinese dictionary.

There is not much milk here.

（3）不定代词的一些惯用法。

1）somebody 表示"大人物"、"要人"；nobody 表示"小人物"、"庸才"。

e.g. In a small town he is somebody, but in a big city he is nobody.

2）something like 有点像。

e.g. He is something like his father.

3）something of 表示"有几分，在某种程度上"。

e.g. He is something of a musician. 他有点音乐知识。

He is something of a sportsman. 他有几分运动员才能。

4）nothing but 只不过，只有（形式上否定，实际上肯定）。

e.g. He is nothing but a policeman. 他只不过是个警察。

I can do nothing but go. 我只好去。

5）anything but 根本不（形式上肯定，实际上否定）。

e.g. She is anything but pretty. 她根本不漂亮。

He is anything but a writer. 他根本不是作家。

八、相互代词

表示相互关系的代词称为关系代词。相互代词有 each other、one another。相互代词无人称、数和格的区别，主要用作宾语。

一般来说，each other 指两者间的相互，而 one another 一般指三个或更多的人或物间的相互。

e.g. John and Mary like each other.

The three men distrusted one another.

九、关系代词

关系代词 who、whom、whose、which、that、as 等可用来引导定语从句。

（1）关系代词在定语从句中的作用。

1）连接定语从句修饰、限定的名词或代词（先行词）和定语从句。

2）代替定语从句所修饰、限定的名词或代词（先行词）。

3）在定语从句中担任一定的句子成分。

在定语从句中，关系代词 who 用作主语；whom 用作宾语；whose 用作定语；而 which 常作主语、谓语动词或介词的宾语。

e.g. The man who is shaking hands with my father is a policeman.

　　Mrs. Smith whom you met yesterday is a friend of mine.

　　This is the scientist whose name is known all over the country.

　　The young man was very happy to get back the gold ring which he had lost on the taxi.

（2）关系代词 that 的特殊用法。

1）that 作为关系代词可取代指人的 who，whom 和指物的 which，分别在定语从句中作主语和宾语。

e.g. People that (who) have no experience cannot do this kind of job.

　　I'd like the car that (which) you bought last year.

2）在 all、much、only 和 anything、everything、nothing、something 等词后，只能用 that、不能用 which、who 等。

e.g. He is the only person that can do it.

　　Everything that he said is wrong.

3）定语从句修饰的名词或代词部分含有序数词或形容词的最高级时，只能用 that。

e.g. He was the first man that danced at the party.

　　The story is the most interesting one that we ever heard.

4）但在非限制性定语从句中和介词后，不能用 that。

e.g. There are 50 students in our class, most of whom are girls.

　　The food, which you put on the desk three days ago, has gone bad.

5）as 也可以引导定语从句，一般用于如下结构：

e.g. I have the same trouble as you (have).

　　As we all know, the 29th Olympic Games will be held in Beijing in 2008.

Exercise 10: 选择填空。

1) They were all very tired, but _____ of them would stop to have a rest.

    A. any   B. some   C. none   D. neither

2) _____ of them knows the reason why the sports meeting is put off.

    A. Every one   B. Everyones   C. Someone   D. All

3) He is a man of _____ words.

    A. little   B. less   C. few   D. fewer

4) The street is beautiful, for there are trees and flowers on _____.

    A. neither side   B. either side

    C. both side   D. all sides

5) Kate is _____ of musician.

    A. anybody   B. anyone   C. something   D. somebody

6) To some life is pleasant, but to _____ it is meaningless.

    A. ones   B. others   C. the other   D. those

7) If you want to change for a double room you'll pay ___ $15.

    A. another   B. other   C. more   D. each

8) _____ is known to all, the Great Wall of China is one of the wonders in the world.

    A. It   B. As   C. That   D. What

9) Meeting my uncle after all these years was an unforgettable moment, _____ I will always treasure.

    A. that   B. which   C. it   D. what

10) After she got married, Lily went to see her mother _____ other week.

    A. each   B. every   C. either   D. neither

Exercise 11: 将下列句子译成英语。

1）我姑姑有两个女儿，一个是护士，一个是演员。

2）还有什么要讨论的吗？没有。

3）今天天气太热了，请再喝一杯冰镇啤酒吧。

4）她不想买冰箱，我也不想买。但我们俩都想买洗衣机。

5）我从没有看见过这么精彩的足球比赛。

Unit 6   Sports & Games
Communicative Samples

Conversation 1

(Xiao Wang and Li Li are going to do exercises.)

Li Li: Xiao Wang, aren't you going to do exercises? It's time, you know.

Xiao Wang: Coming, I'm looking for my sneakers.

Li Li: You're hopeless, always looking for something.

Xiao Wang: I can't help it. That's the way I am.

Li Li: Hey, I didn't notice you have a new tracksuit on. It's nice.

Xiao Wang: It's a present from my sister. Ah, there they are.

Li Li: I'm going to do some bar exercises to build up my muscles. What about you?

Xiao Wang: I plan to go jogging around our campus. Shall we go?

Li Li: Let's go.

Conversation 2

(At the ground.)

Wang Gang: Hi, Xiao Liu! Where have you been?

Xiao Liu: Watching the 100-meter dash.

Wang Gang: Who won?

Xiao Liu: Li Tong, of course. He ran the race in 11.5 seconds. How is Xiao Zhao getting on in the high jump?

Wang Gang: Fine. He's already cleared 1.68 meters. And now it's his turn to jump again. Let's watch a while.

Xiao Liu: All right…. Well done! He's cleared 1.70 meters. And he is the only one left.

Wang Gang: Great! That means our department has got 7 first places already.

Xiao Liu: Let's go and congratulate him.

Wang Gang: Ok.

New Words and Expressions

exercise	/ˈeksəsaiz/	n. & v.	锻炼
sneaker	/ˈsniːkə/	n.	运动鞋
hopeless	/ˈhəuplis/	adj.	没有希望的
tracksuit	/træksuit/	n.	运动服
muscle	/ˈmʌsl/	n.	肌肉
jog	/dʒɔg/	n. & v.	慢跑
campus	/ˈkæmpəs/	n.	校园
dash	/dæʃ/	n. & v.	短跑，赛跑
second	/ˈsekənd/	n. v. & adj.	第二
department	/diˈpɑːtmənt/	n.	部，局，处，科

Exercise 1: Complete the following sentences.

A: Hi, Jim. What's your favorite sport?

B: _____ (足球).

A: Football? I like playing football, too.

B: _____ (世界上很多人都热爱足球).

A: Yes. How about playing football now?

B: _____ (太好了，走吧).

Exercise 2: Fill in the missing letters.

e_erci_ _   sn_ _ke_   hop_le_ _   n_ti_ _   tr_ _ks_ _t

p_ _s_ _t   b_ _ld   m_scl_   j_g   c_mp_s

Paragraph Reading A: Jesse Owens

Jesse Owens was born in a poor, black family in Alabama in 1913. Even when Jesse was a boy, it was clear that he had special athletic ability. He could run extremely fast. In high school he was a long-jump champion.

Jesse's family didn't have enough money to send him to college. However, because he was an excellent athlete, he was able to get a scholarship to Ohio State University track team. In a college track event in 1935, he broke three world records in less than an hour. Owens was chosen for the 1936 U.S. Olympics team. The Summer Olympics were held in Berlin, Germany. At the Olympics, Jesse Owens won both the 100-meter and the 400-meter relay rale. The U.S. relay team won.

Then came the long jump. A German athlete broke the Olympic record. Hitler said that he personally would congratulate the winner. But Owens still had one more jump. He jumped several inches further than the German athlete. Hitler left the stadium in anger, Jesse Owens, a black American, had won his fourth gold medal at the Olympics. Jesse Owens was a hero.

New Words and Expressions

athletic	/æθ'letik/	adj.	运动的
ability	/ə'biliti/	n.	能力
extremely	/iks'tri:mli/	adv.	极端地
long-jump			跳远
champion	/'tʃæmpjən/	n.	冠军
scholarship	/'skɔləʃip/	n.	奖学金
track	/træk/	n. & v.	（赛场的）跑道
choose	/tʃu:z/	v.	选择
relay	/'ri:lei/	n. & v.	接力赛
personally	/'pə:sənəli/	adv.	亲自
congratulate	/kən'grætjuleit/	v.	祝贺
stadium	/'steidiəm/	n.	露天大型运动场
gold	/gəuld/	n. & adj.	黄金，金的

Exercise 3:　**Select the answer that best expresses the main idea of the paragraph reading A.**

1) In high school Jesse Owens _____.

　　A. could run very fast　　　　　　　　B. was a long-jump champion

　　C. set a new record　　　　　　　　　D. was chosen for the U.S Olympics team

2) Jesse Owens was able to get into Ohio State University because _____.

　　A. his parents were able to pay for him

　　B. he was an excellent high school graduate

　　C. his family couldn't send him to a better university

　　D. he could get a scholarship for his special athletic ability

3) When the German Athlete broke the Olympic record, _____.

　　A. Hitler went to congratulate him　　　B. Owens went to congratulate him

　　C. Hitler felt very angry　　　　　　　D. Owens still had one more jump

4) Hitler left the stadium in anger because _____.

　　A. Owens had one more jump

　　B. the German athlete didn't break the Olympic record

　　C. he didn't want to congratulate the German athlete

　　D. the German athlete didn't win gold medal at the Olympics

5) The passage is about _____.

    A. Hitler and the Olympics   B. famous players in Olympic Games

    C. black American athletes   D. a famous American athlete

Exercise 4: Fill in the blanks with words and expressions given below. Change the form where necessary.

hero	born in	personally	stadium	athletic	ability	extremely	champion
congratulate	excellent	scholarship	relay	track	record	medal	

1) My little daughter was _____ December.

2) He is an _____ -looking young man.

3) I don't doubt your _____ to do the work.

4) The army is an _____ complex organism.

5) The _____ is in training for his next fight.

6) This magazine published _____ stories.

7) She has been awarded a _____ to study at Harvard.

8) The dog followed the fox's _____ into the woods.

9) She is rather dim about the importance of keeping _____.

10) The fastest player in a _____ team runs last.

11) He chose Germany, but _____ I'd prefer to go to Spain.

12) We _____ him on his birthday.

13) We will go to the _____ to watch a football match.

14) The soldier earned a _____ for bravery.

15) The real _____ of the match was our goalkeeper.

Exercise 5: Definitions of these words appear on the right. Put the letter of the appropriate definition next to each word.

1) _____ athletic   a. the winner of first prize or first place in a competition

2) _____ champion   b. a large usually roofless building with rows of seats

3) _____ stadium   c. characteristic of athletes or athletics

4) _____ personally   d. money given to a student to help pay for further education

5) _____ scholarship   e. in person

Exercise 6: Translate the following sentences.

Sports and games do a lot of good to our health. They can make us strong, prevent us from getting too fat, and keep us healthy and fit. Especially, they can be of great value to people who work with their brains most of the day, for sports and games give people valuable practice in exercising the body.

Paragraph Reading B: Sports

Around the world more and more people are taking part in dangerous sports and activities. Of course, there have always been people who have looked for adventure – those who have climbed

the highest mountains, explored unknown parts of the world or sailed in small boasts across the greatest oceans. Now, however, there are people who seek an immediate thrill from a risky activity which may only last a few minutes or even seconds.

I would consider bungee jumping to be a good example of such an activity. You jump from a high place (perhaps a bridge or a hot-air balloon) 200 meters above the ground with an elastic rope tired to your ankles. You fall at up to 150 kilometers an hour until the rope stops you from hitting the ground. It is estimated that two million people around have now tried bungee jumping. Other activities which most people would say are as risky as bungee jumping involves jumping from tall buildings and diving into the sea from the top of high cliffs.

Why do people take part in such activities as these? Some psychologists suggest that it is because life in modern society has become safe and boring. Not very long ago, people's lives were constantly under threat. They had to go out and hunt for food, diseases could not easily be cured. Today life offered little excitement. People live and work in a comparatively safe environment; they buy food in shops; and there are doctors and hospitals to look after them if they become ill. The answer for some of these people is to seek danger in activities such as bungee jumping.

New Words and Expressions

dangerous	/ˈdeindʒrəs/	adj.	危险的
activity	/ækˈtiviti/	n.	活动（为兴趣、娱乐等）
adventure	/ədˈventʃə/	n. & v.	冒险
climb	/klaim/	n. & v.	爬
boast	/bəust/	n. & v.	自夸
seek	/siːk/	v.	寻找
immediate	/iˈmiːdjət/	adj.	紧接的
thrill	/θril/	n.	兴奋感、激动、震撼
risky	/ˈriski/	adj.	危险的
bungee	/ˈbʌndʒiː/	n.	蹦极
balloon	/bəˈluːn/	n.	气球
elastic	/iˈlæstik/	adj.	弹性的
ankle	/ˈæŋkl/	n.	踝
hit	/hit/	n. & v.	打击
estimate	/ˈestimeit/	n. & v.	估计
involve	/inˈvɔlv/	v.	包括；涉及

cliff	/klif/	n.	悬崖
psychologist	/saɪˈkɔlədʒist/	n.	心理学者
society	/səˈsaɪəti/	n.	社会
constantly	/ˈkɔnstəntli/	adv.	持续地
threat	/θret/	n.	恐吓，威胁
hunt	/hʌnt/	n. & v.	打猎，搜索
excitement	/ikˈsaitmənt/	n.	刺激，兴奋
environment	/inˈvaiərənmənt/	n.	环境

Exercise 7: Select the answer that best expresses the main idea of the paragraph reading B.

1) A suitable title for the text is _____.

    A. Dangerous Sports: What and Why?   B. The Boredom of Modern Life.

    C. Bungee Jumping: Is It Really Dangerous?   D. The Need for Excitement.

2) More and more people today are _____.

    A. trying activities such as bungee jumping

    B. climbing the highest mountains

    C. coming close to death in sports

    D. looking for adventures such as exploring unknown places

3) In bungee jumping, you _____.

    A. jump as high as you can

    B. slide down a rope to the ground

    C. attach a rope and fall to the ground

    D. fall towards the ground without a rope

4) People probably take part in dangerous sports nowadays because _____.

    A. they have a lot of free time

    B. they can go to hospital if they are injured

    C. their lives lack excitement

    D. they no longer need to hunt for food

5) The writer of the text has a _____ attitude towards dangerous sports.

    A. positive   B. negative   C. neutral   D. nervous

Exercise 8: Fill in the blanks with words and expressions given below. Change the form where necessary.

| offer | environment | dangerous | constantly | unknown | adventure | take part in |
| comparatively | climb | boast | seek | up to | threat | estimate | jump |

1) We all had to _____ the training run, with nobody excepted.

2) Many _____ diseases are carried by insects.

3) _____ stories fired his imagination.

4) The value of imports has _____ sharply in the last year.

5) He was an _____ painter one year ago.

6) Don't believe him; he is just _____.

7) _____ yesterday, I thought he was single.

8) My _____ of the length of the room was 10 feet.

9) She raced to the window to stop the child _____ out.

10) His presence is a _____ to our success.

11) He _____ writes articles for the local paper.

12) He came towards me, smiled and _____ his hand.

13) A land route is _____ safe.

14) Children need a happy home _____.

15) You should _____ advice from your lawyer on this matter.

Exercise 9: Definitions of these words appear on the right. Put the letter of the appropriate definition next to each word.

1) _____ environment　　a. the surrounding conditions

2) _____ adventure　　　b. take part in as a participant

3) _____ estimate　　　 c. an action involving unknown risks or dangers

4) _____ involve　　　　d. judge the approximate value, size, or cost of on the basis of experience

5) _____ society　　　　 e. companionship with one's fellows

Grammar Focus: Number 数词

一、数词的定义和种类

表示数目多少或顺序次第的词叫数词。数词包括基数词和序数词。

二、基数词

（1）表示数目或数量多少的词称为基数词。

（2）基数词词形的表示及特点主要有：

1）1～12 的基数词是独立的单词。

2）13～19 的基数词均以后缀-teen 结尾。

e.g. 13 thirteen　　　15 fifteen　　　19 nineteen

3）20～90 的整十位数词均以-ty 结尾。

e.g. 20 twenty　　　30 thirty　　　40 forty　　　50 fifty

4）几十几的基数词是由十位数词和个位数词合成，中间加连字符"-"。

e.g. 24 twenty-four　　　　　　46 forty-six

5）三位数的数词须在百位与十位（若无十位则和个位）之间加 and。

e.g. 148 one hundred and forty-eight　　206 two hundred and six

6）1000 以上的数字，从后往前数，每三位加一个逗号，第一个逗号前为 thousand，第二个逗号前为 million，第三个逗号前为 billion。

e.g. 2,510 two thousand five hundred and ten

84,296 eighty-four thousand two hundred and ninety-six

274,385 two hundred and seventy-four thousand three hundred and eighty-five

19,326,748 nineteen million three hundred and twenty-six thousand seven hundred and forty-eight

6,364,280,751 six billion three hundred and sixty-four million two hundred and eighty thousand seven hundred and fifty-one

三、序数词

（1）表示数目顺序的词称为序数词。

（2）序数词词形的表示及特点主要有：

1）第 1 到第 19，除第 1—the first，第 2—the second，第 3—the third 外，其余均在基数词后加-th 构成。

e.g. fifth　　　　eighth　　　　ninth　　　　twelfth

2）第 20 到第 90 的整十位序数词是将基数词的词尾 y 变成 ie，再加-th 构成。

e.g. twentieth　　　thirtieth　　　fiftieth　　　eightieth

3）几十几及以上的序数词，其中十位数或百位数、千位数等用基数词，只有个位才用序数词。

e.g. 132 one hundred and thirty-second

四、数词的用法

（1）数词基本上相当于名词和形容词，在句中可作主语、表语、宾语、定语和同位语等。

e.g. The second is bigger than the first.

He was the first to arrive here.

Give me five.

We have six subjects this term.

We two have been to the Great Wall.

（2）在表示"年、月、日"时，"年"用基数词，"日"用序数词。

e.g. 1949 年 10 月 1 日 Oct. the first, nineteen forty-nine

20 世纪 70 年代（1970s）the seventies of twentieth century

（3）表达分数时，先用基数词读分子，再用序数词读分母。当分子大于 1 时，分母要用复数形式的序数词。

e.g. 1/3 one third   5/6 five sixths

（4）编号的事物可用序数词或基数词加名词表示。

e.g. the Fourth Lesson = Lesson Four

　　the fifteenth page = page fifteen

但编号的事物数字较大时，一般用基数词。

e.g. Room 302   page 215   the No. 101 middle school

（5）百分比用基数词＋percent 来表示。

e.g. 50% fifty percent   60% sixty percent

（6）基数词可与表示度量单位的词连用。

e.g. twenty meters deep   ten-meter-long   one hundred yards

（7）有些基数词可构成固定词组。

e.g. one by one 一个个   twos and threes 三三两两

（8）当 hundred、thousand、million 前有具体数字或被 several 修饰时，后面不加-s。

e.g. The newspaper has three million readers.

　　There are several hundred people in the auditorium.

如果这些词以复数形式出现时，则表示"数以百计"、"成千上万"等大概的数量。

e.g. Millions of people will watch the game.

Exercise 10: 选择填空。

1) He is a student of _____.

　　A. Class Second   B. the Class Two

　　C. Class Two   D. Second Class

2) She wrote a _____ composition.

　　A. two-thousand-words   B. two-thousand-word

　　C. two-thousands-word   D. tow-thousands-words

3) About _____ of the workers in that steel works are young people.

　　A. third-fifths   B. three-fifths

　　C. three-fives   D. three-fifth

4) He began to write poems in his _____.

　　A. thirtieth   B. thirty   C. thirty's   D. thirties

5) —When is your birthday?

   —It's on _____.

    A. third March   B. the third of March

    C. three March   D. the three of March

6) He served in the army in _____ when he was in _____.

    A. 1940's; his twenties   B. 1940's; the twenties

    C. the 1940's; his twenties   D. the 1940's; the twenties

7) _____ of the students in our class are from the south.

    A. Two-nineth   B. Two-ninth

    C. Two-ninths   D. Two-nineths

8) I've told him _____.

    A. a hundred time   B. hundred times

    C. hundred of times   D. hundreds of times

9) Do you know when _____ broke out?

    A. Second World War   B. the Second World War

    C. World War Second   D. the World War Two

10) The price was reduced _____.

    A. by 20 percents   B. by 20 percent

    C. by percent of 20   D. on 20 percent

Exercise 11: 将下列句子译成英语。

1）学生们三三两两地走进了教室。

2）十五除三得多少？

3）这所学校三分之一的教师是中年教师。

4）这条河长五百公里，深十米。

5）这个操场比那个操场宽十倍。

Unit 7　People's Life
Communicative Samples

Conversation 1

(Mr. Miller wanted to buy a house and learnt that Mr. Smith had an old house for sale.)

Miller: Here we are, Mr. Smith.

Smith: Oh, the house looks nice. How long have you lived here?

Miller: About forty years. My parents bought it when I was 10.

Smith: That's a long time. Why do you want to sell it?

Miller: My wife died last year, and I sometimes feel lonely and I want to live with my children.

Smith: Where do they live?

Miller: In Los Angeles.

Smith: It's a wonderful place. I like that city very much.

Miller: I know. But it's much more crowded and noisy than this small town.

Smith: Well, how much do you want?

Miller: $ 117,000.

Smith: That's a lot of money. But it's worth that.

Conversation 2

(Anna and Lucy are walking across the park and seeing what other people's doing.)

Lucy: Isn't it a lovely day?

Anna: Yes, it's beautiful.

Lucy: Look that man. What's he doing? Is he working out?

Anna: You mean his exercises? He's doing yoga, I think.

Anna: Look at her! She is jogging.

Lucy: She jogs every morning and she gets up early. She gets up at six and goes jogging.

Anna: What? Every morning. Really?

Lucy: Yes, even on Saturday and Sunday.

Anna: Incredibly.

New Words and Expressions

accompany	/əˈkʌmpəni/	v.	陪伴
worth	/wəːθ/	adj.	有…价值，值…钱
wonderful	/ˈwʌndəful/	adj.	极好的
lonely	/ˈləunli/	adj.	孤独的
beautiful	/ˈbjuːtəful/	adj.	美丽的
yoga	/ˈjəugə/	n.	瑜伽
crowded	/ˈkraudid/	adj.	拥挤的
weekend	/wiːkˈend/	n.	周末
incredibly	/inˈkredəbli/	adv.	不可置信地

Exercise 1: Complete the following sentences.

A: Good afternoon, madam.

B: _____ (午安，先生).

A: Have you any room to rent?

B: _____ (是的，先生，请进来谈吧).

A: Ok，we can talk about some details.

B: _____ (没问题).

Exercise 2: Fill in the missing letters.

s_l_   _cc_mp_ _y   w_ _th   w_nd_ _ful   l_n_ly

b_ _ut _f_l   y_ga   cr_ _ded   w_ _k_ _d   incr_d_bly

Paragraph Reading A: Fire Disaster

Red fire light was seen in the sky and the smoke was rising higher and higher. It was October 8, 1871, the day of the great Chicago Fire. How did this fire begin? No one is sure, but most people blame Mrs. O'Leary's cow. The cow kicked over a lamp and the house began to burn, too. Many of the building there were wooden houses, and they were very dry. More and more buildings burned. There was a strong wind, and the fire crossed the Chicago River and moved farther and farther. Hotels burned. Theatres burned. Ships and schools burned. Millions of dollars and hundreds of people were gone.

But Chicago did not die. Near the lake and to the south, some buildings did not burn. Chicago still had its railways and its port. People built new homes, new shops and new schools. The city continued to grow and grow.

Today it has more than three million people and hundreds of tall buildings. Can you guess what stands in place of Mrs. O'Leary's cow house now? The Chicago Fire Academy.

New Words and Expressions

blame	/bleim/	*n. & v.*	责备
lamp	/læmp/	*n.*	灯
theatre	/'θiətə/	*n.*	剧场
railway	/'reilwei/	*n.*	铁路
continue	/kən'tinju:/	*v.*	继续
grow	/grəu/	*v.*	成长
guess	/ges/	*n. & v.*	猜测

Exercise 3:　Select the answer that best expresses the main idea of the paragraph reading A.

1) The fire broke out probably because of _____.

　　A. the strong wind in winter　　　　B. the dry weather in the city

　　C. a lamp that was kicked over　　　 D. the wooden building there

2) _____ in the south of Chicago were burned.

　　A. Hundreds of people　　　　　　B. Fewer buildings

　　C. More buildings　　　　　　　　D. All the buildings

3) Which of the following if NOT true?

　　A. Not all the people were sure about the cause of the fire.

　　B. The strong wind helped to kill the fire in Chicago.

　　C. Chicago continued to develop after the great fire.

　　D. A fire organization stands in place of Mrs. O'Leary's cow house now.

4) People blame Mrs. O'Leary's cow. The word "blame" means "_____".

　　A. think it is the mistake of　　　　B. catch

　　C. want to kill　　　　　　　　　　D. hate very much

5) Which of the following would be the best title for the passage?

　　A. Development of Chicago After the Fire.

　　B. The Chicago Fire Academy.

　　C. The Great Cow House Fire.

　　D. The Great Chicago Fire.

Exercise 4: Fill in the blanks with words and expressions given below. Change the form where necessary.

blame	fire	kick	lamp	strong	hundreds of	burn	die	building
port	high	dry	smoke	south	continue			

1) The doctor said that he must get rid of _____.

2) After a short break the game _____.

3) Don't _____ on him.

4) Do you see the large _____ over there?

5) He _____ his hand.

6) Flowers will _____ without water.

7) The soil is too _____ to planting.

8) The house was on _____.

9) That table is too _____ for the little girl.

10) The baby was _____ and screaming.

11) The _____ of this country is warmer than the North.

12) _____ children have already been placed with foster families.

13) She could see the rain in the light of the street _____.

14) The ship spent four days in _____.

15) He's _____ enough to lift a car!

Exercise 5: Definitions of these words appear on the right. Put the letter of the appropriate definition next to each word.

1) _____ railway   a. find fault with

2) _____ blame   b. to do the same thing without stopping

3) _____ continue   c. a building for dramatic performances or for showing movies

4) _____ guess   d. rail-road

5) _____ theatre   e. form an opinion from little or no evidence

Exercise 6: Translate the following sentences.

With the development of the Chinese economy, banks began to play a bigger role in people's lives. The bank is no longer a place only for depositing and drawing money. People can also pay the bills for beepers, mobile phones or even tuition at banks. In the banks people can also apply for credit cards or loans to buy houses and cars. The bank has become an indispensable part of the Chinese people's everyday lives.

Paragraph Reading B: Hawaii

Hawaii has been a magic name to people who like to travel. People on both sides of the Pacific Ocean, in Japan and in America, dream of seeing the most beautiful islands in the middle of the ocean. In the tropical lands, the sun drops like a ball of golden fire, into the sea, and it drops so quickly that you can almost see it moving. The sun leaves behind a glow that lights the sky in the quiet water.

People often have a quiet, peaceful time – perfect for a

leisurely walk along the water. This scene is not too different from the dramatic beauty that greeted the first strangers to these islands centuries ago.

They found the beautiful white sand beaches and the waving palm trees, but there were no grand hotels like the ones we see nowadays. The first people came to Hawaii nearly two thousand years ago, but skyscraper hotels were only built in the last 25 years. Now jet airplanes make it possible to fly to Hawaii for a weekend from Tokyo or San Francisco or Los Angeles.

Wherever people come from, they really want to see the original beauty of Hawaii, they want to see the lovely beaches and the mountains called Diamond Head which are almost hidden by the tall hotels.

New Words and Expressions

Hawaii	/hɑːˈwaiiː/	n.	夏威夷
magic	/ˈmædʒik/	n. & adj.	魔法，有魔力的
Pacific Ocean		n.	太平洋
island	/ˈailənd/	n.	岛
tropical	/ˈtrɔpikl/	adj.	热带的
drop	/drɔp/	n. & v.	滴，落下
glow	/gləu/	v.	发光，发热
perfect	/ˈpəːfikt/	adj.	完美的
leisurely	/ˈleʒəli/	adj.	从容不迫的、悠闲的
scene	/siːn/	n.	场面，情景
greet	/griːt/	v.	问候
grand	/grænd/	adj.	盛大的，主要的
skyscraper	/ˈskaiskreipə/	n.	摩天大楼
original	/əˈridʒənəl/	adj.	原作，最初的
hide	/haid/	v.	掩藏，躲藏

Exercise 7: Select the answer that best expresses the main idea of the paragraph reading B.

1) Hawaii is a name _____.

    A. given by people who like to travel

    B. attracting a lot of travelers

    C. with an interesting story behind it

    D. talked about by both Japanese and Americans

2) The most magic thing on these beautiful islands is _____.

    A. the tropical plants

    B. a leisurely walk along the beach

    C. the sunset

    D. the quiet water

3) Which of the following is NOT "the original beauty of Hawaii"?

A.white sand beaches.   B. waving palm trees.

C. tall hotels.   D. the Diamond Head Mountain.

4) The last paragraph suggests _____.

A. the scenery nowadays is different from the original beauty

B. it is not so easy to see the original beauty, because some of the scenery is almost hidden by tall hotels

C. the scenery nowadays is unchanged

D. it is difficult to see the original beauty because things have completely changed in the last 25 years

5) The best topic of the passage is _____.

A. islands   B. Hawaii, A Magic Name

C. traveling in Hawaii   D. the Dramatic Beauty

Exercise 8: Fill in the blanks with words and expressions given below. Change the form where necessary.

magic	dream of	island	in the middle of	tropical	like	golden	quickly
almost	glow	leisurely	scene	be different from	dramatic	greet	

1) She is _____ as tall as her father.

2) I had a _____ glass of beer.

3) _____ in the mountain are particularly beautiful.

4) Platforms in the middle of crowded streets are safety _____.

5) I'd _____ you to go with me.

6) A piece of iron _____ in the furnace.

7) She _____ us by shouting a friendly "Hello".

8) American English is significantly _____ British English.

9) The announcement had a _____ effect on house prices.

10) She _____ running her own business.

11) Businesses have a _____ opportunity to expand into new markets.

12) A passage was cleared through the crowd like _____.

13) They were _____ dinner when I called.

14) He replied to my letter very _____.

15) Many people like to spend their holidays on a _____ island.

Exercise 9: Definitions of these words appear on the right. Put the letter of the appropriate definition next to each word.

1) _____ tropical   a. being entirely without fault or defect

2) _____ perfect   b. a single situation in a play

3) _____ original   c. of or found in the tropics

4) _____ scene   d. an area of land surrounded by water and smaller than a continent

5) _____ island   e. relating to or being the origin or beginning

Grammar Focus: Preposition 介词

一、介词的定义

介词是用来表明名词或代词与其他句子成分间关系的词。

介词也称为前置词，是一种虚词，不能单独担任句子成分，只能用在名词或代词前面。

介词后的成分称为介词宾语。介词和介词宾语一起构成介词短语。

二、介词的主要分类

（1）表示"方向"。

e.g. to、for、towards、up、down、along、across、through、into、out、off、round、around、of、about、throughout、in

（2）表示"位置"。

e.g. at、in、on、by、over、beside、above、under、below、beneath

（3）表示"时间"。

e.g. at、in、on、over、for、through、throughout、from、during、since、till、by、until、before、after

（4）表示"原因"。

e.g. of、from、with、for、through、because of、on account of、owing to、due to

（5）表示"方法"。

e.g. by、with

（6）表示"让步"。

e.g. in spite of、despite、for all、not with standing

（7）表示"关于"。

e.g. with regard to、with respect to、with reference to、as to、as for、regarding、in regard to、concerning、on、about

（8）表示"除外"。

e.g. but、except、except for、with the exception of、besides

（9）表示"标准"、"比率"、"单位价格"。

e.g. by、at、for

三、介词短语的用法

介词短语在句中可充当状语、定语、表语、宾语补足语和主语补足语等。

e.g. Can you write in English?

They are playing basketball on the playground.

The people on the bus are singing.

The boy in front of the desk is Bill.

The machine is out of date.

I consider education of great importance.

They must keep these machines in good condition.

These machines must be kept in good condition.

This book is considered of great use.

四、动词与介词的搭配

（1）相同的动词与不同介词搭配时，有不同的意义。

e.g. Have you *heard from* your parents since they left? （收到来信）

Did you *hear about* the party? （听说）

The accident *resulted in* the death of two passengers. （导致）

His illness *resulted from* malnutrition. （由于）

（2）动词与介词搭配的方式。

1）动词＋介词。

e.g. depend on   approve of   engage in   pay for   rely on   complain about

participate in apply for   fall into   wait for   dream about   aim at

differ from   agree with   object to

2）动词＋宾语＋介词。

e.g. rob…of…   exclude…from…   take…from…

warn…of…   accuse…of…   prevent…from…

remind …of …   inform … of …

3）动词＋副词＋介词。

e.g. look down upon   do away with   come up against   get off with   put up with

go back on   break in on   get along with   go in for   get down to

look forward to   catch up with

五、形容词与介词的搭配

（1）相同的形容词与不同的介词搭配，有不同的意义。

e.g. They are *favorable to* our plan.（赞成）

This kind of weather is *favorable for* swimming.（有利于）

His face is quite *familiar to* me. （为⋯熟悉）

I am still *familiar with* his face. （对⋯熟悉）

（2）有些形容词要求与介词搭配才具有一定的意义。

e.g. Are you *satisfied with* the result?

The students are *fond of* pop music.

These oranges are *inferior to* those I bought last week.

He is still not *accustomed to* the cold weather in Beijing.

六、名词与介词的搭配

（1）某些名词后要求用特定的介词。

e.g. There seems to be no *solution to* this problem.

There has been great *increase in* the production in the last twenty years.

The family background has great *influence on* the family members.

（2）某些名词之前要求用特定的介词。

e.g. *On my way* home, I met my old school classmates.

We sang and danced *to our heart's content*.

Exercise 10: 选择填空。

1) I usually come _____ bus, but today I came on foot.

　　A. in 　　　　　　B. by 　　　　　　C. with 　　　　　　D. on

2) If you are ever in difficulty, don't hesitate to ask _____ my help.

　　A. about 　　　　B. from 　　　　　C. for 　　　　　　D. to

3) John was robbed _____ his money yesterday.

　　A. by 　　　　　　B. from 　　　　　C. with 　　　　　　D. of

4) Have you heard _____ you parents recently?

　　A. from 　　　　　B. of 　　　　　　C. about 　　　　　　D. out of

5) It is not easy to distinguish _____ an American cat and a Canadian cat.

　　A. among 　　　　　　　　　　　　　B. from

　　C. off 　　　　　　　　　　　　　　D. between

6) I can't get used _____ getting up early.

　　A. by 　　　　　　B. for 　　　　　　C. in 　　　　　　D. to

7) Water consists _____ atoms of hydrogen and oxygen.

　　A. of 　　　　　　B. for 　　　　　　C. into 　　　　　　D. to

8) I don't approve _____ children going to bed late.

　　A. on 　　　　　　B. of 　　　　　　C. with 　　　　　　D. to

9) She broke it by accident, she didn't do it _____ purpose.

　　A. at 　　　　　　B. with 　　　　　　C. on 　　　　　　D. in

10) _____ to the station, he bought some books.

    A. On his way   B. By the way

    C. In his way   D. Using the way

Exercise 11：改正用错的介词。

1) The house is built by bricks.

2) We've heard from that movie, but we haven't seen it yet.

3) Helen is suffering by a headache today.

4) Our telephone was out from order and so I couldn't call you.

5) Is this at sale?

Unit 8   Studying Online
Communicative Samples

Conversation 1

(Talking about how to study online.)

Kelly: Tom. Look! I am clicking the website of network campus of Beijing University. We'll enter it soon.

Tom:　What are we going to do at first?

Kelly: Let's look at the introduction information.

Tom:　Click here, we can enter Classroom.

Kelly: Okay, let's have a look.

Tom:　Oh, it's so wonderful; I can choose the grade by myself.

Kelly: Yes, you also can choose the classroom you like better, even your classmates.

Tom:　Do the students also have to take examinations at the end of the term?

Kelly: I don't know for sure. Let's search for information about this.

Tom:　Look here, our classmates also have to take an exam.

Conversation 2

(Having a lesson about the Internet.)

Mary:　Good morning! Do you want to go shopping with me, Crystal?

Crystal: Sorry, I have a lesson today.

Mary:　Today? Don't you know today is Sunday?

Crystal: I know. Have you forgotten I have a lesson on Internet this term?

Mary:　Which subject have you chosen to study?

Crystal: I've chosen the history.

Mary:　It isn't difficult, is it?

Crystal: Yes, it is. Today Professor Li will give us an important lecture.

Mary:　Oh, you must prepare for it.

New Words and Expressions

examination	/ɪɡˌzæmɪˈneɪʃən/	n.	考试
click	/klɪk/	n. & v.	滴答声，点击
website	/webˈsaɪt/	n.	网站；网址
introduction	/ˌɪntrəˈdʌkʃən/	n.	介绍
enter	/ˈentə/	n. & v.	进入
classmate	/ˈklɑːsmeɪt/	n.	同班同学
search	/səːtʃ/	n. & v.	搜寻
message	/ˈmesɪdʒ/	n.	消息
subject	/ˈsʌbdʒɪkt/	n.	科目

Exercise 1: Complete the following sentences.

A: Hi, Peter! _____ (你在干什么呢)?

B: I am searching for some books on the website.

A: Oh, _____ (我不知道如何用计算机去搜索).

B: It's very easy. I can tell you how to use it.

A: Really? Thank you very much.

B: _____ (不用客气).

Exercise 2: Fill in the missing letters.

ex_m_nati_ _　　cl_c_　　　　　w_bsi_e　　intr_d_ _tion　　e_t_r

gr_de　　　　cl_ssm_ _e　　se_r_ _　　　_ess_g_　　　　s_bj_ct

Paragraph Reading A: Internet

We are all busy talking about and using the Internet, but how many of us know the history of the Internet?

Many people are surprised when they find that the Internet was set up in the 1960s. At that time, computers were large and expensive. Computer networks didn't work well. If one computer in the network broke down, the whole network stopped. So a new network system had to be set up. It needed to be good enough to be used by many different computers. If part of the network was not working, information could be sent through another part. In this way the computer network system would keep on working all the time.

At first the Internet was only used by the government, but in the early 1970s, universities, hospitals and banks were allowed to use it, too. However, computers were still very expensive and the Internet was difficult to use. By the start of 1990s, computers became cheaper and easier to use. Scientists had also developed software that made "surfing" the Internet easier.

Today it is easy to get on-line and it is said that millions of people use the Internet every day. Sending E-mails is more and more popular among young people.

The Internet has now become one of the most important parts of people's lives.

New Words and Expressions

surprise	/sə'praiz/	n. & v.	惊奇；使…吃惊
expensive	/iks'pensiv/	adj.	昂贵的
system	/'sistəm/	n.	系统
information	/ˌinfə'meiʃ ən/	n.	信息
cheap	/tʃ i:p/	adj.	便宜的
scientist	/'saiəntist/	n.	科学家
software	/'sɔftwɛə/	n.	软件
send	/send/	v.	送，寄
popular	/'pɔpjulə/	adj.	流行的

Exercise 3:　Select the answer that best expresses the main idea of the paragraph reading A.

1) How long has the Internet been used?

　　A. For about 10 years.　　　　　　　B. For about 20 years.

　　C. For about 40 years.　　　　　　　D. For about 60 years.

2) Which of the following used the Internet first?

　　A. Hospitals.　　　　　　　　　　　B. Universities.

　　C. Banks.　　　　　　　　　　　　 D. The government.

3) Which is true about computers in the 1990s?

　　A. They became cheaper and easier to use.

　　B. They became larger and larger.

　　C. People couldn't buy them anywhere.

　　D. People could get information only from them.

4) What can we infer from the last sentence?

　　A. People will die without the Internet.

　　B. All people should set up their own network.

　　C. People live easily without the Internet.

　　D. People will more and more depend on the Internet.

5) Which is the best title for this passage?

　　A. The History of the Internet.　　　　B. Computers and Information.

　　C. Computers and the Government.　　D. The History of Computers.

Exercise 4: Fill in the blanks with words and expressions given below. Change the form where necessary.

Internet	history	set up	expensive	at that time	network	keep on	software
on-line	hospital	more and more	send	one of	surf	allow	

1) The things in this shop are too _____ for me to buy.

2) Books are not _____ to be taken out of the reading room.

3) These events changed the course of _____.

4) He had to go to _____ for treatment.

5) I wish you wouldn't _____ interrupting me!

6) _____ people are using the Internet.

7) The office _____ allows users to share files and software, and to use a central printer.

8) The data entry terminal is connected to an _____ database while editing is taking place.

9) She _____ the letter by airmail.

10) _____ my friends live in Brighton.

11) I got the information from the _____.

12) A fund will be _____ for the dead men's families.

13) A person who writes computer programs called _____ engineer.

14) I was _____ the net looking for information on Indian music.

15) He was very angry _____.

Exercise 5: Definitions of these words appear on the right. Put the letter of the appropriate definition next to each word.

1) _____ software   a. a person skilled in science and especially natural science

2) _____ system   b. the programs and related information used by a computer

3) _____ information c. the giving or receiving of knowledge or intelligence

4) _____ scientist   d. relating to or coming from the whole body of people

5) _____ popular   e. a group of objects or units combined to form a whole and to
                          move or work together

Exercise 6: Translate the following sentences.

There are 125 million children around the world who do not go to primary school. Two thirds of them are girls. They have to work long hours. They help their families get by. But without education, it is hard to escape the poverty mark. More schooling, textbooks and increased opportunity can break the vicious circle.   Our dream is the world free of poverty.

Paragraph Reading B: How to Read

Are there any good ways to help you read science? Let's consider each of the four rules that you should follow.

1. KEEP YOUR MIND ON WHAT YOU ARE READING. Surely no one can successfully

read a science article or a science textbook and think of other things. Many a car has run through a stop light because a careless driver was thinking of something besides his driving. The same thing is true of reading. It is the most important to think of nothing else while you are reading. Then you will become a better reader.

2. KNOW WHAT YOU READ. The chapter titles and center heads in science text are usually worded in such a way that they arouse your interest and make you want to read. The questions sometimes found at the beginning of the chapters guide you toward the information you want.

3. KNOW THE MEANING OF EVERY WORD. One unknown word can keep you from understanding what you read. Through the use of context clues, word structure rules, and the glossary in your science book you can discover the meaning of most words in the text.

4. FIT YOUR SPEED TO YOUR NEEDS. To get all the important information, you must read slowly and carefully. If you misread them, the experiment may fail, and you may reach wrong conclusions.

New Words and Expressions

rule	/ruːl/	n. & v.	规则
mind	/maind/	n. & v.	意见，注意
surely	/'ʃuəli/	adv.	的确地
successfully	/sək'sesfuli/	adv.	成功地
article	/'ɑːtikl/	n. v. & adj.	文章，商品
careless	/'kɛəlis/	adj.	粗心的
chapter	/'tʃæptə/	n.	章节
title	/'taitl/	n. v. & adj.	标题
arouse	/ə'rauz/	v.	唤醒
context clues			上下文线索
structure	/'strʌktʃə/	n. & v.	结构，建筑
glossary	/'glɔsəri/	n.	术语表；词汇表
discover	/dis'kʌvə/	v.	发现
misread	/mis'riːd/	v.	读错
experiment	/iks'perimənt/	n. & v.	实验
conclusion	/kən'kluːʒən/	n.	结论

Exercise 7:   Select the answer that best expresses the main idea of the paragraph reading B.

1) In the writer's opinion, the first rule for a better reader is you must be _____.

    A. absent-minded   B. glad

    C. attentive   D. low

2) According to the passage, _____ helps you most to read a science book successfully.

    A. fitting your reading speed to your needs

    B. keeping your mind on what you are reading

    C. reading titles and side heads carefully

    D. knowing how to discover the meaning of unknown words

3) Which of the following may not keep you from understanding what you read?

    A. Careless reading.   B. Unknown words.

    C. Mispronounced words.   D. Misreading titles and center heads.

4) If a word that has more than one meaning keeps you from understanding what you read, you'd better use _____ to decide which meaning it has.

    A. a dictionary   B. pronunciation

    C. context clues   D. word structure rules

5) The passage is about how to _____.

    A. make scientific discoveries   B. carry out experiments

    C. read science books or science articles   D. get important information from books

Exercise 8: Fill in the blanks with words and expressions given below. Change the form where necessary.

chapter	way	science	consider	rule	think of	else	successfully	arouse
guide	slow	conclusion	while	in such a way	information			

1) By the end of the _____, you'll have guessed its meaning.

2) The development of modern society depends on _____.

3) I _____ it as a great honour.

4) Be quick, or _____ you'll be late.

5) Her anger was _____ by his rudeness.

6) Instinct is not always a good _____.

7) He is _____ in learning chemistry.

8) _____ I like the colour of the hat, I do not like its shape.

9) This book gives all sorts of useful _____ on how to repair computer.

10) I've come to the _____ that he's not the right person for the job.

11) This explains the _____ under which the library operates.

12) The company has had another _____ achievement.

13) I'm not happy with this _____ of working.

14) You can't speak to your mother _____.

15) When I said that I wasn't _____ anyone in particular.

Exercise 9: Definitions of these words appear on the right. Put the letter of the appropriate definition next to each word.

1) _____ structure   a. something that helps a person find something or solve a mystery

2) _____ arouse   b. the action of building

3) _____ context   c. the parts of something written or spoken that are near a certain word or group of words and that help to explain its meaning

4) _____ clue   d. awaken from sleep

5) _____ conclusion   e. a final decision reached by reasoning

Grammar Focus: Adjective & Adverb 形容词和副词（一）

一、形容词的定义

形容词用来修饰名词或不定代词，表示人或事物的性质、特征、状态或属性。

二、形容词的功用

形容词在句中作定语、表语、宾语补足语、状语。

e.g. The young man likes sports very much.

    A good student must be diligent.

    His success made his parents very happy.

    At last he got home, tired and hungry.

注意："the＋形容词"可转化为名词，在句中作主语和宾语。

e.g. The rich and the poor live in separate sections of the city.

    We should respect the old and love the young.

三、定语形容词的位置

（1）形容词作定语时，一般置于被修饰名词之前。

e.g. The headmaster gave us a helpful report yesterday.

（2）多个形容词同时修饰一个名词时，这些形容词的次序不能随意排列，需遵循一定的规则：

冠词/物主代词/序数词/基数词＋描绘性形容词＋表示形状、大小、长短、高矮的形容词＋表示年龄、新旧的形容词＋表示颜色的形容词＋表示国籍、出处、来源的形容词＋表示材料、物质的形容词＋表示用途、类别的形容词＋被修饰名词。

e.g. the first two paragraphs

    my nice small brown leather bag

    those large round black wooden tables

（3）当被修饰的名词是以-ing、-one、-body 等结尾的合成不定代词时，作定语的形容词需置于这些不定代词后。

e.g. Do you have anything new to tell us?

There is nothing wrong in your homework.

（4）当作定语的形容词后有不定式短语或介词短语时，形容词需置于被修饰的名词之后。

e.g. He is a volunteer worthy of praise.

It is a problem difficult to solve.

四、表语形容词

（1）形容词除作定语外，还可作表语。有些形容词通常不作前置定语，而只作表语。

常见的表语形容词有：afraid、alone、awake、asleep、alive、ashamed、afloat、well、sorry、unable、worth、sure 等。

e.g. The boy is still asleep.

The old man was alone in the house.

（2）常要求带表语形容词的系动词有：be、become、turn、run、go、keep、remain、look、appear、seem、prove、turn out、fall 以及感官动词：feel、smell、sound、taste 等。

e.g. Keep quiet, please.

The book proves very useful.

When the old man entered the room, everybody fell silent.

Her face suddenly went red.

Silk feels soft and smooth.

The beer tastes a little bitter.

五、副词的分类

副词修饰动词、形容词、名词、其他副词或全句。一般分为以下几种：

（1）时间副词：now、then、today、tomorrow、ago、lately、recently、soon、immediately、often、usually、early。

（2）地点副词：here、there、outside、upstairs、anywhere、up、forward、away、in、back、off。

（3）方式副词：simply、quickly、happily、loudly、suddenly、luckily、again、once、easily、together。

（4）程度副词：very、quite、rather、extremely、completely、widely、partly、perfectly、badly、too。

（5）疑问副词：when、where、why、how。

（6）关系副词：when、where、why。

（7）连接副词：when、where、why、how。

（8）其他副词：surely、certainly、really、however、therefore、perhaps、moreover、yes、no。

六、副词的位置

（1）表示确定时间的副词和表示地点的副词一般放在句末。如句中同时有地点和时间副词，地点副词通常在前，时间副词在后。

e.g. They went to the Summer Palace yesterday.

　　She often goes there.

　　I remember having seen him somewhere last year.

（2）表示不确定时间的副词通常放在行为动词之前；但在 be 动词、助动词和情态动词之后。

e.g. He always helps his classmates.

　　She is often the first to come to work.

　　They have already finished their report.

（3）修饰形容词和副词的程度副词，除 enough 外，一般放在被修饰的名词之前。

e.g. He swims quite well.

　　Your little sister is old enough to go to school.

当一句话中作状语的副词出现若干个时，一般的词序是：

频度副词＋程度副词＋方式副词＋地点副词＋时间副词

e.g. He always studies very hard here in the evening.

　　She did her work perfectly there yesterday.

（4）特殊词序：

1）so、as、too、how、however＋形容词＋不定冠词＋单数可数名词

e.g. I have never seen so dirty a room.

　　It is too cold a day.

2）such、what、quite、rather 等＋不定冠词（＋形容词）＋单数可数名词或（＋形容词＋复数名词）或（＋形容词＋不可数名词 ）。

　　e.g. He is really quite a good boy.

　　I have never seen so many books.

3）但当 such 与 all、no、one、few、several、some、any 等连用时，such 应后置，单数名词前不加冠词。

e.g. No such thing has ever happened.

Exercise 10: 选择填空。

1) Oh, boy, why are you killing your time this way? Can't you find something _____ doing at all?

    A. useful   B. valuable   C. worth   D. good

2) —Would you like to join us?

    —Sorry, I'm not _____ as any of you.

    A. so a good player   B. so good a player

    C. a player so good   D. a so good player

3) What he said sounds _____.

    A. nicely   B. pleasant   C. pleasantly   D. wonderfully

4) These apples taste _____ and sell _____.

    A. well; well   B. good; good

    C. good; well   D. well; good

5) He sent me a _____ bag.

    A. black small French leather   B. small black French leather

    C. French leather black small   D. small black leather French

6) _____ to take this course will certainly learn a lot of skills.

    A. Brave enough students   B. Enough brave students

    C. Students brave enough   D. Students enough brave

7) It was raining _____ when we were on our way home.

    A. heavy   B. heavily   C. hardly   D. most

8) I haven't heard from him _____.

    A. late   B. lately   C. recent   D. now

9) We must keep our room clean, for dirt and disease go _____.

    A. hand in hand   B. step by step

    C. from time to time   D. one after another

10) I can not afford _____ computer at present.

    A. so expensive a   B. a such expensive

    C. so an expensive   D. so expensive

Exercise 11: 将下列句子译成英语。

1）她似乎累了。你应该让她好好休息一下。

2）体育锻炼使你愉快而健康。

3）时间到了，下课吧！

4）我去看他时，他已经出去了。

5）春天来了，但是北京的天气依然很冷。

Unit 9   Traffic & Transmission
Communicative Samples

Conversation 1

(Mark has just come back from Beijing, and now he is talking about the traffic in Beijing with Anna.)

Anna: Hi, Mark. Where have you been these days? I haven't seen you for a week.

Mark: I've just come back from Beijing.

Anna: Oh, really. What do you think of Beijing?

Mark: Well, Beijing is a modern city. I'm especially impressed by its efficient traffic system.

Anna: Please tell me more about it.

Mark: The traffic in Beijing is pretty good. You can go everywhere by bus, subway or taxi.

Anna: Is the bus fee expensive?

Mark: No, it is inexpensive. Besides, the subway is cheap, too, and it is fast and comfortable. The taxi is a little expensive, but the driver is very kind to passengers.

Mark: Unbelievable. I'll go there some day to see with my own eyes.

Conversation 2

(Mary will say goodbye to her friend, Lucy at the railway station.)

Mary: I'm very grateful to you for coming to see me off.

Lucy: Not at all. It's the least I can do for a close American friend. By the way, have you bought your ticket?

Mary: Yes, here it is. I got it at the travel agency.

Lucy: Good. Then you're all set. Please excuse me for a moment. I must go and get a few magazines at that stand to read on the train.

(After having bought the magazines)

Lucy: Shall we check in now?

Mary: Yes, let's get on board now to avoid the last minute rush.

Lucy: We've to get on board from platform 3.

Mary: Oh, here's the ticket-counter. Let's get the tickets punched.

Lucy: The train is not in yet.

Mary: Yes, it is. Look! Our train is on this side.

Lucy: Sorry, I was wrong.

Mary: It's all right.

New Words and Expressions

traffic	/'træfik/	n. & v.	交通
impress	/im'pres/	v.	印象
efficient	/i'fiʃənt/	adj.	有效率的
subway	/'sʌbwei/	n.	地铁
comfortable	/'kʌmfətəbl/	adj.	舒适的
passenger	/'pæsindʒə/	n.	乘客
unbelievable	/ˌʌnbi'li:vəbl/	adj.	难以置信的
railway	/'reilwei/	n.	铁道
grateful	/'greitful/	adj.	感激的
magazine	/ˌmægə'zi:n/	n.	杂志
counter	/'kauntə/	n. adv. & prep.	计算器，柜台

Exercise 1: Complete the following sentences.

A: Can I travel from here to the Great Wall by this bus?

B: Yes, sir. _____ (请上车吧).

A: _____ (多少钱)?

B: Fifty Yuan.

A: Here is one hundred Yuan.

B: _____ (先生，这是找您的零钱).

Exercise 2: Fill in the missing letters.

pr_tt_   exp_ _ sive   _ _exp_ _sive   gr_tef_l   st_tion

l_a_t   r_sh   pl_tf_ _m   b_a_d   ag_ _cy

Paragraph Reading A: The Trans–Amazonian Highway

Plans for expanding the road network in Amazonia were drawn up by the Brazilian Government in the 1960s. Initially the roads were to allow access to the area for a small amount of traffic. They will be improved as colonization of the area increases and traffic builds up. Of all the roads, the Trans-Amazonian Highway is the longest and most important. The road starts at Joao Pessoa on the Atlantic coast and crosses the country to meet the roads linking Brazil to Peru and

Bolivia. Its overall length is about 5,300 kilometres.

The main objectives of the High-way are to integrate Amazonia with the areas north and south; promote the colonization of the area and create new agricultural and cattle-raising areas; and to link by land the scattered centres of population on the southern tributaries of the Amazon.

Critics of the project, however, have argued that it might present a grave threat to the ecological balance of the area, the 80,000 indigenous Indians and indeed to the climate of the whole world. Some scientists have gone so far as to predict that deforestation of the area could cause the world's temperature to rise by 2-4 degrees, which in turn would affect the climate of the polar regions and could eventually raise the level of the oceans.

New Words and Expressions

expand	/iks'pænd/	v.	扩张
draw	/drɔ:/	n. & v.	拉
initially	/i'niʃəli/	adv.	最初地
access	/'ækses/	n. & v.	通路；入经
amount	/ə'maunt/	n. & v.	数量
improve	/im'pru:v/	v.	改善
colonization	/ˌkɔlənai'zeiʃən/	n.	殖民
coast	/kəust/	n. & v.	海岸
overall length			全长
objective	/əb'dʒektiv/	n.	目标
integrate	/'intigreit/	v.	结合
promote	/prə'məut/	v.	促进
create	/kri'eit/	v.	创造
agricultural	/ˌægri'kʌltʃərəl/	adj.	农业的
scatter	/'skætə/	v.	分散
tributary	/'tribjutəri/	n. & adj.	（流入大河或湖泊）的支流
project	/'prɔdʒekt/	n. & v.	计划
balance	/'bæləns/	n. & v.	平衡
indigenous	/in'didʒinəs/	adj.	本土的
predict	/pri'dikt/	v.	预知
deforestation	/diˌfɔris'teiʃən/	n.	采伐森林
affect	/ə'fekt/	v.	影响
polar region			极地地区

Exercise 3: Select the answer that best expresses the main idea of the paragraph reading A.

1) We can learn from this passage that the purpose of expanding the road network in the 1960s is to _____.

    A. promote the colonization of the area

    B. improve the traffic network

    C. allow access to the area for a small amount of traffic

    D. link Brazil to Peru and Bolivia.

2) According to the passage, which road is the longest and most important?

    A. Yangtze River.

    B. Amazon.

    C. The Trans-Amazonian Highway.

    D. Nile.

3) The function of the Trans-Amazonian Highway is to _____.

    A. integrate Amazonia with the areas north and south

    B. promote the colonization of the area

    C. create new agricultural and cattle-raising areas

    D. A、B and C

4) According to the passage, which points had critics of the project argued?

    A. It might present a grave threaten to the ecological balance of the area.

    B. It might threat indigenous Indians' lives.

    C. It might affect the climate of the whole world.

    D. A、B and C.

5) The author's tone in this passage is _____.

    A. critical   B. full of praise

    C. doubtful   D. commentative

Exercise 4: Fill in the blanks with words and expressions given below. Change the form where necessary.

level of	affect	region	climate	ecological	critics	draw up	raise
so far as	promote	integrate	improve	area	link	initially

1) The bad weather _____ the growth of crops.

2) In a _____ of political unrest, a dictator can often seize power.

3) He _____ the problem of pollution at the meeting.

4) He was _____ to the position of manager.

5) We must _____ people who come to live here into the community.

6) I want to try my best to _____ my English.

7) Scientists say that there is a certain _____ between smoking and lung cancer.

8) There is heavy traffic in the downtown _____ tonight.

9) She is one of the ruling party's most outspoken _____.

10) The taxi _____ outside the house.

11) We risk upsetting the _____ balance of the area.

12) _____ I am concerned, you can do what you like.

13) The death toll was _____ reported at around 250, but was later revised to 300.

14) People in the _____ should not have travelled to London to fly to the United States.

15) What is the _____ this course?

Exercise 5: Definitions of these words appear on the right. Put the letter of the appropriate definition next to each word.

1) _____ access   a. help (something) grow or develop

2) _____ promote   b. declare in advance

3) _____ predict   c. a condition in which opposing forces are equal to each other

4) _____ deforestation   d. permission or power to enter, approach, or make use of

5) _____ balance   e. the action or process of clearing an area of forests

Exercise 6: Translate the following sentences.

Mr. Smith was looking out of his window, when he saw a truck and a big car hit each other. He ran out to help. There was only one man in the truck and a woman in the car, and neither of them was hurt, but the car was damaged.

Paragraph Reading B: Asking for a Way

A man in the city had a new automobile of which he was very proud. He wanted to try it out, so he drove into the country one afternoon. He drove along admiring the good points of the car without paying any attention to the road. When he finally looked around, he realized that he didn't know where he was, but he kept on driving hoping to find a town or at least a house.

At last, when it was getting dark, he saw a small wooden cottage just off the road. A young boy was chopping wood nearby. The man stopped the car and called out to the boy, "Where does the road go?" "It doesn't go anywhere. It just stays where it is." the boy replied as he went on with his work.

"How far is it to the next town?"

"I don't know. I never measured it," he said.

In a very angry voice the man said, "You don't know anything. You are the biggest fool I have ever seen."

The boy stopped his chopping, looked at the man for a long time, and then said, "I know I don't know anything, but I am not grown up."

New Words and Expressions

automobile	/ˈɔːtəməubiːl/	*n.*	汽车
admire	/ədˈmaiə/	*v.*	赞赏
attention	/əˈtenʃən/	*n.*	关心；注意
realize	/ˈriəlaiz/	*v.*	认识到
wooden	/ˈwudn/	*adj.*	木制的
chop	/tʃɔp/	*n. & v.*	砍
voice	/vɔis/	*n. & v.*	声音

Exercise 7: Select the answer that best expresses the main idea of the paragraph reading B.

1) Then man got lost because _____.

    A. he was in a strange country

    B. he wasn't thinking about where he was driving

    C. someone gave him wrong directions

    D. there were no towns

2) The man thought his new car _____.

    A. might cause accidents   B. was the latest model

    C. was pretty good   D. might get damaged

3) The man met the boy _____.

    A. in the city   B. in the late afternoon

    C. at midday   D. when he was nearly mad

4) After asking a couple of questions, the man _____.

    A. became angry   B. thought the boy was funny

    C. laughed at the boy   D. drove on

5) The young boy was _____.

    A. quite healthy   B. very informative

    C. quite helpful   D. not at all informative

Exercise 8: Fill in the blanks with words and expressions given below. Change the form where necessary.

grow up	anything	for a long time	angry	measure	never	chop	how far
proud	realize	dark	call out	finally	without	automobile	

1) Is this watch _____ like the one you lost?

2) She was very _____ that they didn't call him.

3) A meter is a _____ of length.

4) _____ forget to lock the door at night.

5) The cook _____ the meat up before cooking it.

6) Our team feels _____ that it has won every match this year.

7) You'll _____ your mistakes sooner or later.

8) That the litter girl is afraid of the _____.

9) After several delays, the plane _____ left at six o'clock.

10) He drove away _____ saying goodbye.

11) This traffic jam is caused by an _____ accident.

12) You need to _____ an engineer to help you solve this problem.

13) If you're good you can eat with the _____.

14) I haven't seen you _____.

15) Could you tell me _____ is it to the nearest hospital.

Exercise 9: Definitions of these words appear on the right. Put the letter of the appropriate definition next to each word.

1) _____ admire   a. a usually four-wheeled vehicle with its own power system

2) _____ automobile   b. to cut into small pieces

3) _____ chop   c. to look at with admiration

4) _____ realize   d. the act or power of fixing one's mind upon something

5) _____ attention   e. be aware of

Grammar Focus: Adjective & Adverb 形容词和副词（二）

七、形容词和副词的比较等级和比较结构

形容词、副词的比较等级分为：原级、比较级和最高级。

（1）原级的用法。

1）表示被比较双方在性质、特征、状态、程度等某一方面相等时，用 as … as 结构，意为"…和…一样"。

e.g. He is as tall as his brother.

It is as cold today as it was yesterday.

He speaks French as fluently as you.

This car runs as fast as that one.

2）表示被比较双方在性质、特征、状态、程度等某一方面不相等时，用 not so (as) … as 结构，意为"…不如…"或"…没有…"。

e.g. There are not so (as) many seats in this hall as in that hall.

She doesn't look so beautiful as her sister.

（2）比较级和最高级的形式和用法。

1）单音节形容词和副词是在词尾加-er 和-est。

e.g. kind – kinder – kindest   fast – faster – fastest

2）三音节或三音节以上的形容词和副词是在原级前加 more 和 most。

e.g. difficult – more difficult – the most difficult

beautifully – more beautifully – most beautifully

3）双音节形容词和副词的变化是个习惯问题，即有的词是在词尾加-er、-est；有的词是在原级前加 more、most。

e.g. happy – happier – happiest   clever – more clever – most clever

4）两个人或事物进行比较时，用比较级。

基本句式：

①主语＋系动词＋形容词比较级＋than＋对比成分

②主语＋行为动词＋副词比较级＋than＋对比成分

e.g. This parcel is heavier than that one.

It rains more often in Wuhan than in Xi'an.

5）三个或三个以上的人或事物进行比较时，用最高级。

基本句式：

①主语＋系动词＋the＋形容词最高级＋（名词）＋表示范围的短语或从句

②主语＋行为动词＋副词最高级＋（名词）＋表示范围的短语或从句

e.g. Shanghai is one of the biggest cities in the world.

She is the eldest among the three sisters.

Mr. Chen works most carefully in our group.

（3）比较级的特殊用法。

1）表示倍数的常用句型：… times as＋原级＋as …

e.g. This table is 3 times as big as that one.

This dictionary costs twice as much as that one.

2）可用 much、far、by far、even、a lot、a little、a great deal、a good deal 等程度副词来修饰形容词和副词的比较级和最高级，表示"更…"、"…得多"等含义。

e.g. The student study even harder than before.

The bridge being built now is by far the longest across the river.

还可用"名词 / 数词词组＋比较级"表示"比…相差多少"。

e.g. My younger sister is a head shorter than I.

I got to the cinema ten minutes later than Wang.

This piece of cloth is an inch longer than that one.

3）the＋比较级，the＋比较级，表示"越…越…"。

e.g. The more productions you sell, the more money you'll get.

The longer you stay, the better it will be.

4）比较级＋and＋比较级，表示"越来越…"。

e.g. Summer is coming, it is getting hotter and hotter.

5）the＋比较级＋of the two＋名词，表示两者之中较怎么样。

e.g. He is the younger of the two brothers.

She is the more beautiful of the two sisters.

6）more than、less than 的一些惯用法。

①修饰数量词，前者表示"多于…"，后者表示"少于…"。

e.g. More than 5,000 workers went on strike.

This pen costs me less than 2 dollars.

②用于形容词和副词前，前者表示"非常"，后者表示"很不"。

e.g. We are more than glad to hear the good news.

The doctor is very busy and less than pleased to treat the patient.

③more…than…表示"与其说…不如说…"。

e.g. To me, she is more enemy than friend.

与其说她是我朋友，不如说她是我敌人。

④no more than 表示"只有"；not more than 表示"至多，不超过"。

e.g. There were no more than six boys in our class.

They have made not more than five kinds of model machines.

注意：

e.g. He is no more stupid than that girl. 他和那女孩一样聪明。

He is not more stupid than that girl. 他不像那女孩那样笨。

This food is no worse than that. 这食物同那种食物一样好吃。

7）否定＋比较级＝最高级

e.g. He has never spent a more worrying day.

他过了最担心的一天。

There is no greater love than that of a man who lays down his life for his friend.

为朋友而放弃生命的人的爱是最伟大的爱。

Exercise 10: 选择填空。

1) —Did you have a good sleep last night?

—Yes, I never sleep _____.

    A. badly   B. better   C. separately   D. lively

2) If there were no examinations, we should have _____ at school.

    A. much happiest time   B. a more happier time

    C. a much happier time   D. the happiest time

3) Canada is larger than _____ country in Asia.

    A. any   B. any other   C. other   D. another

4) The Yellow River is the second _____ river in China.

    A. long   B. longer   C. longest   D. the longest

5) He made the _____ mistakes in the dictation.

    A. less   B. least   C. fewer   D. fewest

6) So far as I am concerned, education is about learning and the more you learn _____.

    A. the more for life are you equipped

    B. the more equipped for life you are

    C. the more life you are equipped for

    D. you are equipped the more for life

7) My _____ brother is three years _____ than I.

    A. older; older   B. older; old   C. elder; elder   D. elder; older

8) In recent years, travel companies have succeeded in selling us the idea that the further we go _____.

    A. our holiday will be better   B. our holiday will be the better

    C. the better our holiday will be   D. the better will our holiday be

9) She is _____ older than she looks.

    A. a lot of   B. very   C. quite   D. far

10) After the new technique was introduced, the factory produced _____ cars in 2002 as the year before.

    A. as many twice   B. as twice many

    C. twice many as   D. twice as many

Exercise 11: 将下列句子译成英语。

1）英语同数学一样重要。

2）王东比我大两岁，但我比他高一个头。

3）"世界贸易中心"是世界上最大最高的建筑之一。

4）你学习得越多，你获得的知识也就越广。

5）这条河比那条河宽而深。

Unit 10　Letters
Communicative Samples

Conversation 1

(Mrs. Smith wants to mail two letters to her friends in England. She goes into the post office.)

Clerk: Good afternoon, Madam, What can I do for you?

Smith: I'd like to mail these two letters to England.

Clerk: Sure. It's thirty cents for each half-ounce letter. Let's weigh your letters first. That's two dollars ten cents.

Smith: Well, how long does it take to get to England?

Clerk: It's about four or five days.

Smith: Four or five days?

Clerk: That's right.

Smith: Could I send them by express?

Clerk: Of course. But you have to pay another two dollars.

Smith: That's fine.

Conversation 2

(Diana and Tony were in the room, waiting for their mails.)

Diana:　I hear the sound of a bicycle bell just outside of our door. It might be the postman.

Tony:　Maybe. It's time to get our mail. Let me have a look.

Diana:　Is it the postman? I've been waiting for a letter from my uncle in Japan.

Tony:　Yeah. Hello, Mr. Martin, are there letters for us?

Martin:　Yes, you get two letters and a card. Heres one for you. Diana, there is a letter for you.

Diana:　Where is it from?

Martin:　It's mailed from Tokyo.

Diana and Tony: Thank you. See you.

Martin: A pleasure. Bye.

New Words and Expressions

mail	/meil/	n. & v.	邮件
cent	/sent/	n.	美分
ounce	/auns/	n.	盎司
weigh	/wei/	v.	重
dollar	/'dɔlə/	n.	美元
postman	/'pəʊstmən/	n.	邮差

Exercise 1: Complete the following sentences.

A: Excuse me. _____ (我要寄一封信).

B: You can put it into the pillar box.

A: _____ (多少邮资) is for a local letter?

B: Local postage is usually twenty cents.

A: _____ (非常感谢).

B: You're welcome.

Exercise 2: Fill in the missing letters.

m_ _l   c_n_   o_nce   w_ _gh   e_pr_ss

d_ll_ _   p_stm_n   c_u_se   p_st   off_ce

Paragraph Reading A: Pen Friends

> Moorfield,
> High lane,
> Haslemere, Suttey.
> England.
> 2nd   October

Dear Tom,

I want a pen friend. My teacher gave me your name and address. She said you wanted a pen friend too. I am 21.I live in a small town in England. It's called Haslemere. It's not far from London. I like collecting stamps, playing football and watching TV. I'm learning to play the piano but I hate practicing. Please write to me soon.

                              Tony Williams

336 Western Avenue,

Berkeley,

California 99867,U.S.A.

3rd December

Hi there Tony!

It's sure good to have a real English pen friend. I like your letter. I'm 22. I live in California. It's usually warm and sunny. I like making things. The other kids and I are building a tree house. Al is my best friend. He's helping me, but he's a bit dumb. I have two sisters. They look like this. We fight a lot. Pop and me are the only boys round here.

Bob Krefeld

P.S How do you play football in England?

New Words and Expressions

collect	/kə'lekt/	v. adj. & adv.	收集
stamp	/stæmp/	n.	邮票
piano	/pi'ɑːnəu/	n.	钢琴
practice	/'præktis/	n.	练习
kid	/kid/	n.	小孩
fight	/fait/	n. & v.	打架；打斗
December	/di'sembə/	n.	十二月

Exercise 3: Select the answer that best expresses the main idea of the paragraph reading A.

1) According to the first letter, why does Tony Williams write this letter?

A. Because he has got Tom's name and address.

B. Because Tom is his friend.

C. Because he wants to make a pen friend with Tom.

D. Because Tom asks him to write this letter.

2) We can learn from the first letter that Tony's hometown is _____.

A. Berkeley   B. California

C. Haslemere   D. London

3) According to the second letter, how does Tom respond to Tony's letter?

A. Happiness.   B. Anger.   C. Indifferent.   D. Hostility.

4) Which of the following sentences is NOT ture?

A. Tony is 22 years old.   B. Tom is 22 years old.

C. Tom likes making things.   D. Tony likes collecting stamps.

5) It can be inferred from these two letters that _____.

    A. Tony like collecting stamps, playing football and watching TV

    B. Tom didn't like Tony

    C. Tom and Tony will make friends with each other

    D. Tom is the only boys round there

Exercise 4: Fill in the blanks with words and expressions given below. Change the form where necessary.

England	October	a bit	teacher	address	small	dumb	far from
collect	stamp	watch	piano	hate	fight	practice	

1) After a long time journey I feel _____ tired.

2) He is my history _____.

3) This box is too _____, Do you have a larger one?

4) The class remained _____ when the teacher asked a question.

5) We are _____ money for the famine victims.

6) When you want to mail a letter you need to put a _____ on the envelope.

7) The man is being _____ by the police.

8) She plays the _____ well.

9) She looked at her opponent with _____ in her eyes.

10) The two hooligans had a _____ in the street.

11) What's your name and _____?

12) The National Day is on _____ 1st.

13) The people of _____ used to mean the British.

14) Computers, _____ destroying jobs, can create employment.

15) He usually wants to _____ his English on me.

Exercise 5: Definitions of these words appear on the right. Put the letter of the appropriate definition next to each word.

1) _____ practice   a. to bring or come together into one body or place

2) _____ stamp   b. device or instrument for stamping

3) _____ collect   c. a repeated or usual action

4) _____ fight   d. to act for or against

5) _____ kid   e. a young person

Exercise 6: Translate the following sentences.

In one 24-hour period, new births number in China is about 52,056 while death, in the same period is about 12,960 for a net population increasing per day of 39,096. In the 365 days of the calendar year on average, these figures show that 14.27 million will currently be added to China's population each year. This means that, if the current rate of population expansion continues, China's present-day population will double in size in next 84 years.

Paragraph Reading B：Fun at the Supermarket

22 Newport Avenue,
London, S.E.28
24th October

Dear Dora,

How nice it was to hear from you. Tummy's asleep and at last I've managed to find a quiet moment to write to you.

I must tell you about an embarrassing experience I had yesterday - I know you'll laugh! I was shopping at a supermarket and I had Timmy with me. He was following me round the shop as I filled my basket. When I went to the cash desk to pay I got a surprise. My basket was full of strange things. "I didn't put these things in the basket," I said to the assistant, pointing at three packets of dog biscuits. Suddenly we both looked at Timmy who was smiling innocently and we realized what had happened. He had put the things in my basket while we were going round together. I turned to pay and there was a loud crash!

There was a display of packets of washing-powder near me, and of course, Timmy had pulled out a packet from the bottom of the pile …

New Words and Expressions

moment	/ˈməumənt/	n.	片刻
embarrass	/imˈbærəs/	v.	使困窘
supermarket	/ˈsjuːpəˌmɑːkit/	n.	超级市场
cash desk		n.	付款台
assistant	/əˈsistənt/	n. & adj.	助手，辅助的
innocently	/ˈinəsnt/	adv.	无辜地
biscuit	/ˈbiskit/	n.	饼干
crash	/kræʃ/	n. & v.	碰撞
packet	/ˈpækit/	n. & v.	包装

Exercise 7: Select the answer that best expresses the main idea of the paragraph reading B.

1) According to the letter, why did the author write this letter to her friend?

A. Because she was very happy when she received her friend's letter.

B. Because she would like to tell her friend an embarrassing experience.

C. Because she thought the experience yesterday would make her friend laugh.

D. Because she had nothing to do after.

2) The word "embarrass" in third line can be replaced by _____.

   A. angry   B. uncomfortable   C. shy   D. funny

3) The passage implies that the little boy is _____.

   A. naughty   B. foolish   C. troublesome   D. strange

4) What happened when she went to the cash desk for paying?

   A. Timmy put the candy in my basket.

   B. My basket was filled with strange things.

   C. Timmy was lost.

   D. I cannot find my purse.

5) What's the main idea of this letter?

   A. Shopping in the supermarket.   B. An embarrassing experience.

   C. A naughty boy.   D. Funny story.

Exercise 8: Fill in the blanks with words and expressions given below. Change the form where necessary.

from the bottom of	experience	asleep	full of	biscuit	pull out	display
nice	manage	moment	embarrass	laugh	put …in	crash	pile

1) He told us about his _____ in Africa.

2) My arm is _____, probably because I've been lying on it.

3) Don't eat too much _____, it'll do harm to your health.

4) You've got us into a _____ mess.

5) We finally _____ to get there in time.

6) His story was so funny that the people present couldn't help _____.

7) The young man was _____ by lack of money.

8) The stock market _____ of 1929 ruined many people.

9) We put the old newspapers in _____ on the floor.

10) The screens will _____ the user name in the top right-hand corner.

11) My suitcase was _____ books.

12) He thought for a _____ before replying.

13) A car suddenly _____ in front of me.

14) Did you _____ sugar _____ my coffee?

15) I found some French coins _____ my bag.

Exercise 9: Definitions of these words appear on the right. Put the letter of the appropriate definition next to each word.

1) _____ cash   a. cause to feel self-consciously confused or distressed

2) _____ embarrass   b. break with violence and much noise

3) _____ assistant   c. a person who assists another

4) _____ crash   d. freely from guilt or blame

5) _____ innocently   e. money in the form of coins or bills

Grammar Focus: Tense 时态（一）

一、时态的定义和种类

英语的时态就是用谓语动词来表示动作在不同的时间的发生或以不同的表现方式存在的状态。

英语时态包括时（time）和式（form）两个方面。

时表示动作发生或状态存在的时间。有现在、过去、将来和过去将来四种时间。

式是表示动作或状态的表现方式。有一般、进行、完成和完成进行四种方式。

每一种时和式的结合就构成一种时态。

英语动词共有 16 种时态。

现以 be 动词、have 动词及行为动词 make 为例，列表如下：

动词 be 的常用时态变化。

一般现在	一般过去	一般将来
I am	I was	I shall / will
You are	You were	You will
He ⎫	He ⎫	He ⎫
She ⎬ is	She ⎬ was	She ⎬ will
It ⎭	It ⎭	It ⎭
We ⎫	We ⎫	We shall / will
You ⎬ are	You ⎬ were	You will
They ⎭	They ⎭	They will
过去将来	现在完成	过去完成
I should / would	I have been	I had been
You would	You have been	You had been
He ⎫	He ⎫	He ⎫
She ⎬ would	She ⎬ has been	She ⎬ had been
It ⎭	It ⎭	It ⎭
We should / would	We ⎫	We ⎫
You would	You ⎬ have been	You ⎬ had been
They would	They ⎭	They ⎭

动词 have 的常用时态变化。

一般现在	一般过去	一般将来
I have	I had	I shall / will have
You have	You had	You will have
He She } has It	He She } had It	He She } will have It
We You } have They	We You } had They	We shall / will have You will have They will have
过去将来	现在完成	过去完成
I should / would have	I have had	I had had
You would have	You have had	You had had
He She } would have It	He She } has had It	He She } had had It
We should / would have You would have They would have	We You } have had They	We You } had had They

行为动词的常用时态变化（以 make 为例）。

	一般式	进行式	完成式	完成进行式
现在	make, makes	am / is / are making	have / has made	have / has been making
过去	made	was / were making	had made	had been making
将来	shall / will make	shall / will be making	shall / will have made	shall / will have been making
过去将来	would make	would be making	would have made	would have been making

二、一般现在时

（1）定义：一般现在时通常表示经常发生的或习惯性的动作或目前的状态。

（2）构成：大多以动词原形表示；主语为第三人称单数时，通常在动词后加-s 或-es（其变化规则同名词单数变复数的规则相同）。

e.g. work – works   learn – learns   come – comes

    pass – passes   wash – washes   teach – teaches

    fix – fixes   go – goes

be 动词和动词 have 的变化参看上表。

（3）用法。

1）表示现状、性质、状态和经常的或习惯性的动作；常用的时间状语有：often、sometimes、usually、always、seldom、in the morning、every day、on Sunday。

e.g. The students have sports at four every afternoon.

Every culture has its own way to show love.

The 21st century is the century of information technology.

Do you like art music or pop music?

2）表示不受时间限制的事实或普遍真理。

e.g. The teacher told the students that the sun rises in the east.

Five plus three is eight.

Light travels faster than sound.

October 1st is our National Day.

3）在时间和条件状语从句中可用一般现在时代替一般将来时。

e.g. She will go to see him as soon as he arrives.

I'll stay at home if it rains tomorrow.

4）表示已安排或计划好的、将来必定会发生的动作或存在的状态，一般多用 be、come、go、arrive、leave、start、fall 等动词。

e.g. My birthday falls on July 24th.

His train leaves at 6:30 tomorrow afternoon.

The meeting is at 9:00; Don't be late.

She comes back tonight.

Exercise 10: 选择填空。

1) My mother _____ Mrs. Quite well. They were introduced at a party.

　　A. is knowing　　　　　　　　　B. was knowing

　　C. knows　　　　　　　　　　　D. had been knowing

2) No one _____ where he has hidden the money.

　　A. knows　　　　B. know　　　　C. have known　　　　D. is known

3) Please bring me some books next time when you _____.

　　A. will come　　　B. come　　　C. have come　　　　D. are coming

4) This kind of cloth _____ well.

　　A. washes　　　　　　　　　　B. wash

　　C. is washed　　　　　　　　　D. is washing

5) The food you bought yesterday _____.

　　A. is tasted good　　　　　　　B is tasted well

　　C. tastes good　　　　　　　　D tastes well

Exercise 11: 将下列句子译成英语。

1）他们每天晚上看电视。

2）我坐飞机走，明天下午六点到那儿。

3）你多久给你的妈妈发一封邮件？

4）你的朋友看起来很年轻。

5）他一回来就叫他给我打电话。

Exercise 12: 用动词适当的形式填空。

The world we _____ (live) in _____ (be) a big, big round ball. It is turning all the time, but you cannot _____ (see) or _____ (feel) this turning. There _____ (be) other worlds, too, but the one we _____ (live) on is called the earth. It is made of soil and rock, trees and grass, air and water, and all the other things around you.

The sun _____ (shine) on the earth, the rain _____ (fall) on it, the wind _____ (blow) over it. The sun _____ (shine) on you, the rain _____ (fall) on you, and the wind _____ (blow) your hat off. You _____ (live) on the earth, and everything around you _____ (be) part of it.

Unit 11　Energy Resources
Communicative Samples

Conversation 1

(Alisa and Kevin are talking about reuse resources.)

Alisa:　Hi, Kevin. You know that our modern world has become a "throwaway" society.

Kevin: What does it mean?

Alisa:　It means that people are encouraged to consume as much as possible and waste materials at will.

Kevin: Yes. I think most people forget that earth's recourses are exhaustible.

Alisa:　That's right. People should realize this situation and try to reverse this trend.

Kevin: What shall we do about it?

Alisa:　It's very easy. People should realize the importance of resource conservation.

Kevin: You mean what?

Alisa:　We should make our efforts to cherish our planet's limited recourses.

Kevin: You're absolutely right.

Conversation 2

(Essex and Amelia are talking about how to protect the natural recourses.)

Essex:　Do you know how to protect the natural recourses, Amelia?

Amelia: The key to this is the reuse of materials in our everyday life.

Essex:　Could you tell me some details?

Amelia: Ok. For one thing, we should buy products in reusable containers.

Essex:　That's a good idea. Anything else?

Amelia: We should not get rid of the old things we don't need.

Essex:　Exactly. Throwing all the old things away is a bad habit.

Amelia: We can also dispose of properly used materials. For example, books, cans, batteries, etc.

Essex:　How can we deal with them?

Amelia: We can take them to the flea markets.

Essex:　Great.

New Words and Expressions

reuse	/ˌriːˈjuːz/	n. & v.	再使用；再利用
encourage	/inˈkʌridʒ/	v.	鼓励
consume	/kənˈsjuːm/	v.	消费
cherish	/ˈtʃeriʃ/	v.	珍爱
natural	/ˈnætʃərəl/	adj.	自然的
container	/kənˈteinə/	n.	容器
dispose	/disˈpəuz/	v.	处置；处理
battery	/ˈbætəri/	n.	电池

Exercise 1: Complete the following sentences.

A: Hi, Alisa. _____ (你知道怎么保护水资源吗)?

B: I think the key to this is to reduce the waste.

A: _____ (是的。还有其他的办法).

B: _____ (什么办法)?

A: We can build sewage-treatment plants so that we can reuse the water.

B: _____ (不错的主意)!

Exercise 2: Fill in the missing letters.

r_s_u_ce   s_c_e_y   m_ter_ _l   s_t_ _ti_n   tr_ _d

d_t_ _l   h_b_t   fl_ _   m_rke_   r_d

Paragraph Reading A: Recycling Waste

European countries are now making an active effort to reuse materials more than they used to. This is called recycling. Materials such as paper, glass or metal are collected, sorted, treated and used again. Old papers are recycled. The ink is taken out by a special technique, and new paper is made. Oil from factories and motor oil can be treated and reused. In many cities in Europe rubbish is collected separately. Empty glass bottles are collected, and the glass is broken and reused for making new bottles.

Developing countries all over the world already recycle materials. In India, waste paper is collected, sorted and recycled. Paper bags are made from unsold newspapers. In Egypt, waste is collected by rubbish cars and sorted. Leftover food is given to pigs and vegetable matter is put back onto the fields. In some Asian countries, shoes are made from the rubber of old car tyres.

The Chinese government is also working hard against pollution. More than 60,000 small factories which seriously polluted the environment were shut down in 1996. Many materials like used rubber gloves, glass bottles, cans and other containers are treated or recycled. However, no single country can save the environment alone.

New Words and Expressions

European	/ˌjuərəˈpi(ː)ən/	adj. & n.	欧洲的，欧洲人
effort	/ˈefət/	n.	努力
reuse material		n.	再生资源
recycle	/riːˈsaikl/	n. & v.	再循环
ink	/iŋk/	n.	墨水
technique	/tekˈniːk/	n.	技术
rubbish	/ˈrʌbiʃ/	n.	垃圾
separately	/ˈsepərətli/	adv.	分开地；个别地
empty	/ˈempti/	adj.	空的
Egypt	/ˈiːdʒipt/	n.	埃及
leftover	/leftˈəuvə/	n. & adj.	剩余物
glove	/glʌv/	n.	手套
single	/ˈsiŋgl/	n. & adj.	单一的
alone	/əˈləun/	adv. & adj.	单独的

Exercise 3: Select the answer that best expresses the main idea of the paragraph reading A.

1) What's the main topic of this passage?

　　A. Oil from factories and motor oil can be treated and reused.

　　B. Waste is collected by rubbish cars and sorted in some countries.

　　C. Many countries are now trying their best to reuse materials.

　　D. Developing countries all over the world already recycle materials.

2) The first paragraph concerns that ＿＿＿＿.

　　A. new bottles can be made of broken glass

　　B. european countries are now paying more attention to reuse materials more than they used to

　　C. in many cities in Europe rubbish is collected separately

　　D. the reuse of materials such as paper, glass or metal is called recycling

3) How did people recycle materials in India?

　　A. Waste is collected by rubbish cars and sorted.

　　B. Leftover food is given to pigs.

　　C. Waste paper is collected, sorted and recycled.

　　D. Vegetables matter is put back onto the fields.

4) Which of the following sentences is NOT mentioned in this passage?

    A. Materials such as paper, glass or metal are collected, sorted, treated and used again.

    B. Developing countries all over the world already recycle materials.

    C. The Chinese government is also working hard against pollution.

    D. In some European countries, shoes are made from the rubber of old car tyres.

5) It can be inferred from this passage that _____.

    A. China can solve the problem of waste

    B. all countries must work together to save the environment

    C. all old things can be reused in the future

    D. more than 60,000 small factories in China were shut down in 1996

Exercise 4: Fill in the blanks with words and expressions given below. Change the form where necessary.

such as	reuse	shut down	effort	used to	waste	rubber	however
single	separately	technique	treat	material	pollution	work hard	

1) Don't forget to _____ the computer when you don't need it.

2) Many of his _____ failed in the end.

3) It's a _____ of time to wait any longer.

4) Rub out the pencil marks with a _____.

5) _____ hard he tries, he can't win the game.

6) Why did you _____ me out for praise?

7) It's a pity that her mother _____ her badly.

8) What _____ is this dress make of?

9) We must reduce levels of environmental _____.

10) In order to save expenses, please _____ your envelopes.

11) They were photographed _____ and then as a group.

12) Her _____ has improved a lot over the past season.

13) I'm not _____ eating so much at lunchtime.

14) Opportunities _____ this did not come every day.

15) To make a promotion, you must _____.

Exercise 5: Definitions of these words appear on the right. Put the letter of the appropriate definition next to each word.

1) _____ recycle   a. hard work of mind or body

2) _____ material   b. the manner in which details are treated

3) _____ container   c. something into which other things can be put

4) _____ technique   d. the substance of which something is made or can be made

5) _____ effort   e. process in order to regain materials for human use

Exercise 6: Translate the following sentences.

A new report says the world's supply of fresh water is in danger. The warning was given by the World Commission on Water for The Twenty-first Century. The group was established to study the conditions of the world's supply of fresh water.

Problems with the world's freshwater supply affect wildlife as well as people. In 1998, twenty-five million people became refugees from environmental disasters as a result of flooding, pollution and other water problems.

Paragraph Reading B: How to Solve the Energy Shortage

Energy shortage is a very serious problem in the world. Many people worry that energy resources will be exhausted if we use them in an unchecked way. This will cause serious problems and even crisis and jeopardize the survival of mankind.

The problem can be solved in one way or another. One is to conserve and save our energy. Most countries have realized the wastefulness in their using of energy. They are trying to conserve energy. For example, some countries have a daylight saving system to use less electricity for lighting. Some cities have enforced water savers in public such as restrooms and bars. By these means, people hope the drain on energy resources could be slowed down.

However, conservation alone cannot solve the problem. Another way is to develop new energy resources. Obviously, no matter how hard we try to save energy resources and how abundant they are, we will use them up sooner or later. There are many energy resources that we can develop and utilize. We don't have to depend only on the current conventional energy resources. There are many other energy resources that we can develop such as nuclear power, waterpower and solar power. These resources, if developed, can completely replace conventional energy and thus solve the problem of energy shortage.

New Words and Expressions

shortage	/ˈʃɔːtidʒ/	n.	短缺，匮乏
resource	/riˈsɔːs/	n.	资源
exhaust	/igˈzɔːst/	v.	用尽
unchecked	/ʌnˈtʃekt/	adj.	未受制止的
jeopardize	/ˈdʒepədaiz/	v.	危害
survival	/səˈvaivəl/	n.	幸存
wastefulness	/ˈweistfulnis/	n.	浪费
electricity	/ilekˈtrisiti/	n.	电流
enforce	/inˈfɔːs/	v.	强制执行

drain	/dreɪn/	n.	排水沟
abundant	/əˈbʌndənt/	adj.	丰富的
utilize	/juːˈtɪlaɪz/	v.	利用
current	/ˈkʌrənt/	adj.	当前的
conventional	/kənˈvenʃənl/	adj.	常规的
nuclear power		n.	核动力
solar	/ˈsəʊlə/	adj.	日光的

Exercise 7: Select the answer that best expresses the main idea of the paragraph reading B.

1) Which of the following best states the theme of the passage?

A. Energy shortage will cause serious problems and even crisis and jeopardize the survival of mankind.

B. There are many ways to solve energy shortage problem.

C. Energy shortage is a very serious problem in the world.

D. People adopt a daylight saving system to save energy.

2) The author states all the following except that _____.

A. most countries have realized the wastefulness in their using of energy

B. we must depend only on the current conventional energy resources

C. conservation alone cannot solve the problem of the energy shortage

D. there are many energy resources that we can develop and utilize

3) According to the author, which of the ways to solve the problem of energy shortage is not mentioned?

A. We can develop atomic energy.

B. We can develop alternative energy such as nuclear power, waterpower and solar power.

C. We can use a daylight saving system to use less electricity for lighting.

D. Some cities have enforced water savers in public places such as restrooms and bars.

4) People must develop new energy resources because _____.

A. energy shortage will cause crisis

B. most countries have realized the wastefulness in their using of energy

C. we will use energy resources up in the future

D. they think energy shortage is a very serious problem in the world

5) The author's tone in this passage is _____.

A. indifference   B. worry   C. disappointment   D. advisory

Exercise 8: Fill in the blanks with words and expressions given below. Change the form where necessary.

| depend on | energy | slow down | shortage | worry | resource | exhaust | jeopardize |
| survival | mankind | utilize | sooner or later | for example | conventional | solar |

1) Such work demands much _____.

2) Don't _____ about your future.

3) Oil is the most important natural _____ in Kuwait.

4) He is _____ by the questions.

5) They hope to find new resources for _____.

6) The earth is a part of the _____ system.

7) She's very _____ in her views.

8) He was the sort of person you could _____.

9) There is a similar word in many languages, _____ in French and Italian.

10) He would never do anything to _____ his career.

11) There is no _____ of things to do in the town.

12) The car _____ as it approached the junction.

13) His only chance of _____ was a heart transplant.

14) _____ you will have to make a decision.

15) The resources at our disposal could have been better _____.

Exercise 9: Definitions of these words appear on the right. Put the letter of the appropriate definition next to each word.

1) _____ resource   a. occurring in or belonging to the present time

2) _____ current   b. the act or fact of living or continuing longer than another person or thing

3) _____ shortage   c. following, agreeing with, or based on convention

4) _____ survival   d. a new or a reserve source of supply or support

5) _____ conventional   e. a lack in the amount needed

Grammar Focus: Tense 时态（二）

三、一般过去时

（1）定义：一般过去时表示过去时间里发生的动作或存在的状态。

（2）构成：由动词的过去式表示。

1）规则动词的过去式是在动词原形后加-ed 或-d。

e.g. want – wanted   open – opened   play – played

     live – lived   hope – hoped   move – moved

     study – studied   cry – cried   try – tried   carry – carried

     stop – stopped   beg – begged   permit – permitted

2）不规则动词的过去式有其特殊形式，须逐个记忆。

e.g. beat – beat   become – became   catch – caught

     feel – felt   go – went   meet – met   sell – sold

     tear – tore   grow – grew   hide – hid   see – saw

（3）用法。

1）表示过去某一时刻或某一段时间内发生的动作或存在的状态，通常与表示过去的时间状语连用，如 a few minutes ago、yesterday、last Sunday 等。

 e.g. The train arrived ten minutes ago.

  What time did you get up yesterday morning?

  They were in Canada in 2005.

2）表示过去经常或反复发生的习惯性动作。

 e.g. When I was a little girl, I often went to play in that park.

  He used to smoke a lot.

  They always went to work by bus.

四、一般将来时

（1）定义：一般将来时表示将来发生的动作或存在的状态。

（2）构成：由助动词 shall 或 will＋动词原形构成，其中 shall 多和第一人称搭配。

  一般将来时除了上述形式外，还有"be going to ＋动词原形"；"be to＋动词原形"和"be about to＋动词原形"，这些结构在用法上有差别，详见用法说明。

（3）用法。

1）结构"shall / will＋动词原形"通常表示单纯的将来。

 e.g. They will leave for Beijing the day after tomorrow.

  He will be back in a few days.

  Where shall we meet this evening?

  I shall be twenty years old next year.

  但此种结构也有其他含义。will 常表示"决心"、"意愿"；shall 用于第二人称时，表示说话者的将来意愿或允诺。

 e.g. I will work hard to support my family.

  He won't do it.

  Shall I open the window for a while?

  You shall have the book.

2）"be going to＋动词原形"多用于口语中所有人称，表示主语打算在最近或将来要做某事。这种打算往往是事先考虑好的。

 e.g. I'm going to meet Tom at the station at six.

  When are you going to finish your work?

  We are going to call a meeting to discuss it.

  这种结构还可以表示说话人根据已有的迹象认为即将发生某事。

e.g. Look at these black clouds—it is going to rain.

I am afraid I am going to have a bad cold.

3）"be to＋动词原形"表示职责、义务、意图、约定、可能性等，可以带时间状语。

e.g. You are to be back by 10 o'clock.

There is to be a sports meeting on Saturday.

We are to meet at the school gate.

4）"be about to＋动词原形"表示即将做某事，一般不跟时间状语。

e.g. We are about to leave.

The parade is about to start now.

（4）可以替代一般将来时的其他时态。

1）一般现在时可用来表示已安排或计划好将来必定会发生的动作或存在的状态，一般多用于 come、go、arrive、leave、start、fall 等动词。

e.g. We leave Beijing at 9 p.m. tomorrow and arrive in Nanjing at 7 a.m. the day after tomorrow.

When do you start on the tour?

2）现在进行时可用来表示按计划即将发生的动作，多与表示移动的动词 come、go、arrive、leave、fly、start 等连用。

e.g. He is leaving for London.

Christmas is drawing near.

They aren't coming.

I am seeing him tomorrow.

Exercise 10: 选择填空。

1) My aunt _____ to see us. She'll be here soon.

　　A. came　　　　　　　　　B. is coming

　　C. comes　　　　　　　　　D. had come

2) The last half of the nineteenth century _____ the steady improvement in the means of travel.

　　A. has witnessed　　　　　　B. was witnessed

　　C. witnessed　　　　　　　　D. is witnessed

3) I _____ Alexander in the park the other day.

　　A. have met　　　B. met　　　C. had met　　　D. was meeting

4) When I was young, I _____ horses every day.

　　A. am used to ride　　　　　B. used to riding

　　C. used to ride　　　　　　　D. was used to ride

5) —When are you going to visit your uncle in Chicago?

   —As soon as _____ our work for tomorrow.

   A. we're complete   B. we'd complete

   C. we'll complete   D. we complete

Exercise 11: 将下列句子译成英语。

1）昨晚他到车站去给他们送行。

2）我给了他一个忠告。

3）我上中学的时候总是六点钟起床。

4）我不打算在这儿待很久。

5）布朗先生今天下午来喝茶。

Exercise 12: 用动词适当的形式填空。

Yesterday, I _____ (not wake) up until 8:00 a.m. I _____ (get) up immediately and _____ (get) dressed. I _____ (have) breakfast and _____ (leave) my house at 8:45. I _____ (be) an hour late and _____ (not get) to work until 9 o'clock. I _____ (work) all day and _____ (not have) lunch. I _____ (finish) working at 7:30 p.m. and _____ (go) home at 8 p.m. I _____ (be) two hours late and _____ (not have) dinner until 9 o'clock. After dinner I _____ (read) the newspaper for a while and _____ (make) some telephone calls. I _____ (listen) to the radio for two hours and _____ (go) to bed at midnight. I _____ (not go) to sleep immediately. I _____ (sleep) just six hours last night. I _____ (not sleep) very well.

Unit 12   How to Learn
Communicative Samples

Conversation 1

(Tom and Jim are Talking about in the Professor Wang's study.)

Tom: Jim, Professor Wang has a big collection of books in his study, hasn't he?

Jim:　That' true. Just imagine, he has read all of them! When I talk to him about books, I feel that he has pored over every book that I have ever heard of.

Tom: Here are some modern English Classics. Have you read any of them?

Jim:　Almost none, I'm afraid. What about you?

Tom: Er.., I was fond of English writers when I was only a school boy.

Jim:　Who are the well-known twentieth-century English writers?

Tom: Oh, they are John Galsworthy, G B. Shaw, and also T.S. Elliot.

Jim:　T.S. Elliot? Wasn't he an American?

Tom: He was born in the United States, but he chose British nationality later…

Jim:　I see.

Conversation 2

(Miller and Rose are talking about reading.)

Miller: Rose, I notice, Mr. Li, the Chinese are very fond of reading.

Rose:　Exactly.

Miller: Lots of people read in the underground trains and on buses.

Rose:　You are quite right.

Miller: Personally I think there's nothing better than reading a good book after a day's work.

Rose:　It's excellent relaxation, too.

Miller: And there is a saying, "It's never too late to learn."

Rose:　Yes, reading is a good way to learn.

Miller: I wish I had more time for reading.

New Words and Expressions

professor	/prə'fesə/	n.	教授
collection	/kə'lekʃən/	n.	收藏
imagine	/i'mædʒin/	v.	想象
pore	/pɔː/	v.	熟读
classics	/'klæsiks/	n.	杰作
nationality	/ˌnæʃə'næliti/	n.	国籍
fond	/fɔnd/	adj.	喜爱的
excellent	/'eksələnt/	adj.	卓越的
relaxation	/ˌriːlæk'seiʃən/	n.	放松
absolutely	/'æbsəluːtli/	adv.	绝对地

Exercise 1: Complete the following sentences.

A: What do you think of English?

B: _____ (很难学).

A: If you want to learn English well, you must remember a lot of words.

B: _____ (是啊，但是这门课对我来是说太难了).

A: I know how you feel. But I think you should stick with it.

B: _____ (我知道了，谢谢你).

Exercise 2: Fill in the missing letters.

c_ll_ _tion   c_ _tur_   p_ _fess_ _   i_ _gi_e   cl_ssi_s

f_ _d   afr_ _d   p_ _son_lly   r_lax_tion   ex_ _lle_t

Paragraph Reading A: Vast, West or Vest

One day, Mary read a sentence, from "English for Beginners", in which "the vast deserts of America" were referred to. Mr Parkhill soon discovered that poor Mary did not know the meaning of "vast". "Who can tell us the meaning of 'vast'?" asked Mr Parkhill lightly.

Tom's hand shot up, volunteering wisdom, He was all proud grins. Mr Parkhill, in the rashness of moment, nodded to him.

Tom rose, radiant with joy, " 'Vast'! It's commink from direction, Ve have four directions: de naut, de sot, de heast, and de vast."

Mr Parkhill shook his head. " Er - that is 'west', Tom." He wrote "VAST" and "WEST" on the blackboard. To the class he added, tolerantly, that Tom was apparently thinking of "west", whereas it was "vast" which was under discussion.

This seemed to bring a great light into Tom's inner world. "So is 'vast' that you asking?"

Mr Parkhill admitted that it was "vast" for which he was asking.

"Aha!" cried Tom. "You minn 'vast', not"—with sscorn—" 'vast' ."

"yes," said Mr Parkhill, faintly.

"Hau Kay!" said Tom, essaying the vernacular. "Ven I'm buying a suit of clothes, I'm gettink de cawt, de pants, an'de vast!"

New Words and Expressions

beginner	/bi'ginə/	*n.*	初学者
vast	/vɑ:st/	*adj.*	巨大的
lightly	/'laitli/	*adv.*	轻轻地
volunteer	/vɔlən'tiə/	*n. v. & adj.*	志愿者，志愿的
wisdom	/'wizdəm/	*n.*	智慧
grin	/grin/	*n. & v.*	露齿笑
rashness	/ræʃnis/	*n.*	轻率
nod	/nɔd/	*n. & v.*	点头
radiant	/'reidjənt/	*adj.*	发光的
shake	/ʃeik/	*n. & v.*	摇动
west	/west/	*n. adv.*	西方
blackboard	/'blækbɔ:d/	*n.*	黑板
tolerantly	/'tɔlərənt/	*adj.*	容忍的
whereas	/wɛər'æz/	*conj.*	然而
discussion	/dis'kʌʃən/	*n.*	讨论
essay	/'esei/	*n. & v.*	企图，散文
vernacular	/və'nækjulə/	*adj.*	本国的
vest	/vest/	*n. & v.*	汗衫

Exercise 3: Select the answer that best expresses the main idea of the paragraph reading A.

1) The writer probably felt that _____.

    A. Tom can answer the question

    B. Tom is very clever

    C. Tom made a misunderstanding about the word "vast"

    D. Mary knows the meaning of "vast"

2) According to the passage, what does the word "vast" mean?

    A. endless.   B. big.

    C. extensive.   D. broad.

3) Why did Tom raise his hand and answer the question?

    A. Because he was confident.

    B. Because he wanted to show off his knowledge.

    C. Because he knew the meaning of "vast".

    D. Because he was clever.

4) It can be inferred that this story happened _____.

    A. in the lecture   B. in the classroom

    C. in the dining hall   D. in the film

5) The author's tone in this passage is _____.

    A. critical   B. humorous   C. neutral   D. hate

Exercise 4: Fill in the blanks with words and expressions given below. Change the form where necessary.

sentence	beginner	refer to	soon	discover	vast	west	vest
wisdom	radiant	volunteer	direction	discussion	essay	a suit of	

1) This _____ is wrong.

2) His book for the _____ in English is a best seller.

3) I'll _____ come back.

4) Columbus _____ America in 1492.

5) The sun sets in the _____.

6) I would question the _____ of borrowing such a large sum of money.

7) She _____ to search for the missing child.

8) We asked a policeman and he gave us _____ to Buckingham.

9) The students were asked to write _____ about the importance of education.

10) After considerable _____, they decided to accept out offer.

11) She was _____ with health.

12) The victims were not _____ by name.

13) His business empire was _____.

14) The weather become colder and colder, and I want to buy a cotton _____.

15) _____ clothes mean a jacket and trousers or a skirt.

Exercise 5: Definitions of these words appear on the right. Put the letter of the appropriate definition next to each word.

1) _____ vast   a. very great in extent, size, amount, degree, or intensity

2) _____ tolerantly   b. relating to, or using ordinary especially spoken language

3) _____ essay   c. showing tolerance

4) _____ vernacular   d. a wise attitude, belief, or course of action

5) _____ wisdom   e. a usually short written work giving a personal view on a subject

Exercise 6: Translate the following sentences.

I'd like to speak Chinese, so I bought whatever Chinese tapes and videos I could find and listened to them over and over again. I had conversations with my Chinese friends, and I would tape our conversations. Every night I went to bed listening to these tapes … In this way, I was hearing and speaking Chinese for up to 4 to 5 hours a day.

Paragraph Reading B: Marking on Books

When we read a book, we often mark it. That is to say, we often circle or underline the important sentence. How to mark a book is very important. Here are some ways of marking a book intelligently and fruitfully.

NO.1. Underlining: of major points, of important or forceful statements.

NO.2. Vertical lines at the margin: to emphasize a statement already underlined.

NO.3. Star, asterisk, or other marks at the margin: to be used economically, to emphasize the ten or twenty most important statements in the book.

NO.4. Numbers in the margin: to indicate the sequence of points the author makes in developing a single argument.

NO.5. Numbers of other pages in the margin: to indicate where else in the book the author made points related to the point marked; to tie up the ideas in a book, which, though they may be separated by many pages, belong together.

NO. 6. Circling: of key words or phrases.

NO. 7. Writing in the margin, or at the top or bottom of the pages: for the sake of recording questions (and phrase answer) which a passage raised in your mind; reducing a complicated discussion to a simple statement; recording the sequence of major points right through the books. I use the end papers at the back of the book to make personal index of the author's points in the order of their appearance.

New Words and Expressions

mark	/mɑ:k/	n. & v.	标记
circle	/ˈsə:kl/	v.	圈出
intelligently	/inˈtelidʒəntli/	adv.	聪明地
fruitfully	/ˈfru:tfuli/	adv.	成果丰硕地，富有成效地
emphasize	/ˈemfəsaiz/	v.	强调
economically	/i:kəˈnɔmikəli/	adv.	经济地
indicate	/ˈindikeit/	v.	指出
sequence	/ˈsi:kwəns/	n.	次序

single	/'sɪŋgl/	n. & v.	个别的；一对一的；真诚的
argument	/'ɑ:gjumənt/	n.	争论
tie up			绑好，占用
phrase	/freɪz/	n. & v.	短语
sake	/seɪk/	n.	缘故
complicate	/'kɔmplɪkeɪt/	v.	（使）变复杂
index	/'ɪndeks/	n. & v.	索引

Exercise 7: Select the answer that best expresses the main idea of the paragraph reading B.

1) From the third device for marking a book, we can guess that the Chinese meaning of the word "economically" should be _____.

    A. carelessly   B. carefully   C. not wasteful   D. mostly

2) The author tells us that the purpose of writing numbers of other pages in the margin is _____.

    A. trying up the ideas belonging together in a book

    B. emphasizing the statements

    C. indicating the points

    D. developing the arguments

3) How to deal with the key words and phrases in the marking a book according to the passage?

    A. We should circle them.   B. We must write them down.

    C. We need to underline them.   D. We can draw vertical lines.

4) Why does the reader need to write in the margin, or at the top or bottom of the page?

    A. Recording questions or answers in his mind.

    B. Changing a complicated discussion into a simple statement.

    C. Recording the major points right through a book.

    D. Doing all the above.

5) How does the author deal with the blank space at the back of the book?

    A. To write what he has learned from the book.

    B. To write a diary.

    C. To draw an outline of the book.

    D. To discuss the argument governed by the author of the book.

Exercise 8: Fill in the blanks with words and expressions given below. Change the form where necessary.

| circle | vertical | appearance | tie up | sequence | complicate | in one's mind | major |
| margin | fruitfully | mark | indicate | through | at the top of | underline | |

1) The plane _____ around the airport before landing.

2) The cliff rose in a _____ wall from the sea.

3) He _____ the importance of unit in his speech.

4) He had the _____ of being unhappy.

5) He escaped defeat by a narrow _____.

6) I do not wish to _____ the task more than is necessary.

7) Research _____ that eating habits are changing fast.

8) We have encountered _____ problems.

9) Prices are _____ on the goods.

10) These problems are all _____, you know.

11) He described the _____ of events leading up to the robbery.

12) The burglar got in _____ the window.

13) He left his dog _____ to a tree.

14) She was screaming _____ her voice.

15) For a lesson to be _____ taught, the teacher must make thorough preparations before going to class.

Exercise 9: Definitions of these words appear on the right. Put the letter of the appropriate definition next to each word.

1) _____ sequence　　　　　a. operating with little waste or at a savings

2) _____ complicate　　　　b. to point out or point to

3) _____ emphasize　　　　c. to place emphasis on

4) _____ economically　　　d. make or become complex or difficult

5) _____ indicate　　　　　e. a continuous or connected series

Grammar Focus: Tense 时态（三）

五、过去将来时

（1）定义：过去将来时表示从过去某一时间来看将要发生的动作或存在的状态。多用于宾语从句中。

（2）构成：由助动词 should 或 would＋动词原形构成，其中 should 多和第一人称搭配。

过去将来时除了上述形式外，还有 "was / were going to ＋动词原形"；"was / were to＋动词原形" 和 "was / were about to＋动词原形"，这些结构在用法上有差别，详见用法说明。

（3）用法。

1）would / should＋动词原形单纯表示过去将来。

e.g. He said he would go to Shanghai for the holiday.

　　I told him I would see him off at the station.

　　He promised me that I should succeed.

2）was / were going to＋动词原形，表示过去曾经打算或准备要做的动作。

e.g. They were going to have a meeting.

The students were going to plant some trees around the playground.

此结构也可以表示过去很有可能发生的动作。

e.g. I thought it was going to rain.

3）"was / were to＋动词原形"和"was / were about to＋动词原形"这两种结构可以表示某种过去将来的意义。

e.g. We were to finish the work in three days.

I was about to go out when a friend dropped in.

The train was about to leave.

六、现在进行时

（1）定义：现在进行时表示说话时正在发生或进行着的动作。

（2）构成：am / is / are＋现在分词（动词＋ing）。

一般情况下，现在分词的构成是在动词词尾加-ing。

e.g. go – going   see – seeing   stay – staying

have – having   live –living   take – taking

cut – cutting   run – running   stop – stopping

die – dying   lie – lying   tie – tying

（3）用法。

1）表示此时此刻正在进行的动作，常与表示"此时此刻"的时间状语 now、at this moment、at this time 等连用。

e.g. The children are reading magazines in the library at the moment.

Is it raining now?

Those people are looking at the picture.

2）表示现阶段正在进行而说话时不一定正在进行的动作。

e.g. My mother is making a dress these few days.

She is translating a novel.

Are you working hard this term?

3）常与副词 always、continually、constantly 等连用，表示反复出现的或习惯性动作，含有说话人的赞扬、不满、讨厌、遗憾等情绪。

e.g. The girl is always smiling happily.

You're always making the same mistake.

She is constantly changing her mind.

4）表示事物发展的过程。

e.g. Winter has come. It's getting colder and colder.

The leaves on the trees are turning yellow.

She is finding out that chemistry is quite difficult.

5）可用来表示按计划即将发生的动作，多与表示移动的动词 come、go、arrive、leave、fly、start 等连用。

e.g. What are you doing next Friday?

I'm going for a walk, are you coming with me?

John is coming to see me next week.

（4）一般现在时和现在进行时的主要区别。

1）一般现在时表示经常性动作，现在进行时表示现在或现阶段正在发生的动作。

e.g. He studies hard. 他（经常）努力学习。

He is studying hard. 他（此刻或现阶段）正在努力学习。

2）一般现在时表示现在发生的动作，现在进行时表示眼前看得见的动作。

e.g. Boats pass under the bridge. 船从桥下穿过。

The boat is passing under the bridge. 船正从桥下穿过。

3）一般现在时不带感情色彩，现在进行时常带感情色彩。

e.g. John does fine work at school. 约翰在学校成绩优秀。（事实）

John is constantly doing fine work at school. 约翰在学校总是成绩优秀。（赞扬）

4）不表示持续的行为，而表示知觉、感觉、看法、认识、感情、愿望或某种状态的动词通常不用现在进行时。这种用法的动词有：see、hear、smell、taste、recognize、notice、forget、remember、understand、know、believe、suppose、mean、think、feel、love、hate、care、like、wish、hope、refuse、have、be、seem、look…

Exercise 10：选择填空。

1) He said that he _____ the information for all the computers soon.

　　A. gets　　　　B. would get　　　　C. has got　　　　D. had got

2) He's always _____ money and forgetting to pay you back.

　　A. borrow　　B. borrowing　　　　C. borrowed　　　　D. been borrowed

3) He wondered whether I _____ the birthday party the next day.

　　A. will attend　　　　　　　　B. attended

　　C. had attended　　　　　　　D. would attend

4) Mary has come to see you. She _____ for you downstairs at the moment.

　　A. is waiting　　　　　　　　B. was waiting

　　C. has been waiting　　　　　D. has waited

5) He _____ with a special pen just because he likes to be different.

　　A. has always written　　　　B. is always writing

　　C. would always write　　　　D. will always write

6) Selecting a mobile telephone for personal use is no easy task because technology _____

so rapidly.

　　A. is changing　　　　　　　B. changed

　　C. will have changed　　　　　D. will change

Exercise 11: 将下列句子译成英语。

1）那些人都懂英语，他们在谈什么？

2）我在这儿等公共汽车，我总是乘公共汽车上班。

3）噢，又下雨了！这里每年这个时候常下雨吗？

4）头儿说我们很快就要离开了。

5）外国使节将要会见总统。

Exercise 12: 用动词适当的形式填空。

My name _____ (be) Walter. My sister's name _____ (be) Mary and my brother's name _____ (be) Leo. I _____ (speak) French pretty well and a little Chinese.

Actually, my native language _____ (be) English. I _____ (study) French right now. my sister Mary _____ (write) a letter to a friend of hers in South America. Her friend _____ (be) an engineer. He _____ (speak) Spanish. He _____ (study) English now but he _____ (not speak) English very well yet. I _____ (not remember) his name. At the moment, my brother Leo _____ (read) a magazine. The magazine _____ (be) in French. Leo _____ (read) French very well, and he _____ (speak) exceptionally well. Right now, I _____ (think) about my Chinese lesson. I _____ (have) a lot of trouble with my pronunciation. I _____ (speak) Chinese with an American accent.

Glossary

A

ability	/ə'biliti/	n.	能力	6A
absolutely	/'æbsəlu:tli/	adv.	绝对地	12
abundant	/ə'bʌndənt/	adj.	丰富的	11B
access	/'ækses/	n.	通路，入径	9A
accident	/'æksidənt/	n.	事故	2A
accompany	/ə'kʌmpəni/	v.	陪伴	7
accounting	/ə'kauntiŋ/	n.	会计学	1A
activity	/æk'tiviti/	n.	活动	6B
address	/ə'dres/	n. & v.	地址	3B
admire	/əd'maiə/	v.	赞赏	9B
adult	/ə'dʌlt/	n. & adj.	成人，成人的	1A
adventure	/əd'ventʃə/	n. & v.	冒险	6B
affect	/ə'fekt/	v.	影响	9A
Africa	/'æfrikə/	n.	非洲	2A
agricultural	/,ægri'kʌltʃərəl/	adj.	农业的	9A
Alaska	/ə'læskə/	n.	阿拉斯加州	2A
alone	/ə'ləun/	adv. & adj.	单独的	11A
amount	/ə'maunt/	n. & v.	数量	9A
animal	/'æniməl/	n.	动物	2A
ankle	/'æŋkl/	n.	踝	6B
appearance	/ə'piərəns/	n.	外貌，外观	1B
approve	/ə'pru:v/	v.	批准	5A
argument	/'a:gjumənt/	n.	争论	12B
arouse	/ə'rauz/	v.	唤醒	8B
arrange	/ə'reindʒ/	v.	安排	5B
article	/'a:tikl/	n. v. & adj.	文章，商品	8B
assistant	/ə'sistənt/	n. & adj.	助手，辅助的	10B
athletic	/æθ'letik/	adj.	运动的	6A
attention	/ə'tenʃən/	n.	注意	5
attention	/ə'tenʃən/	n.	关心；注意	9B
attentively	/ə'tentivli/	adv.	注意地	1B
attract	/ə'trækt/	v.	吸引	4A
automobile	/'ɔ:təməubi:l/	n.	汽车	9B
avoid	/ə'vɔid/	vt.	避免	1A

B

balance	/ˈbæləns/	n. & v.	平衡	9A
balloon	/bəˈluːn/	n.	气球	6B
battery	/ˈbætəri/	n.	电池	11
beach	/biːtʃ/	n.	海滩	4A
beautiful	/ˈbjuːtəful/	adj.	美丽的	7
beef	/biːf/	n.	牛肉	1
beginner	/biˈginə/	n.	初学者	12A
biscuit	/ˈbiskit/	n.	饼干	10B
blackboard	/ˈblækbɔːd/	n.	黑板	12A
blame	/bleim/	n. & v.	责备	7A
boast	/bəust/	n. & v.	自夸	6B
bookmark	/ˈbukmɑːk/	n.	书签	3B
bound	/baund/	adj.	一定会，很可能会	1B
bridge	/bridʒ/	n.	桥	2B
browser	/ˈbrauzə/	n.	浏览器	3B
bungee	/ˈbʌndʒiː/	n.	蹦极	6B
business	/ˈbiznis/	n.	商业，事情	3B
cabbage	/ˈkæbidʒ/	n.	卷心菜	1

C

California	/kæliˈfɔːnjə/	n.	加利福尼亚	4A
campus	/ˈkæmpəs/	n.	校园	6
canteen	/kænˈtiːn/	n.	食堂；餐厅	1
career	/kəˈriə/	n.	事业，生涯，速度	1A
careless	/ˈkɛəlis/	adj.	粗心的	8B
cash desk		n.	付款台	10B
cause	/kɔːz/	n. & v.	原因	2A
celebrate	/ˈselibreit/	v.	庆祝	5B
cent	/sent/	n.	美分	10
champion	/ˈtʃæmpjən/	n. & v.	冠军，拥护	6A
change	/tʃeindʒ/	n. & vt.	改变	1A
chapter	/ˈtʃæptə/	n.	章节	8B
chat	/tʃæt/	n. & v.	聊天	3A
cheap	/tʃiːp/	adj.	便宜的	8A
check	/tʃek/	n. & v.	阻止，核对	3A
chemical	/ˈkemikəl/	n. & adj.	化学的	2A
cherish	/ˈtʃeriʃ/	v.	珍爱	11

choose	/tʃuːz/	v.	选择	6A
chop	/tʃɔp/	n. & v.	砍	9B
circle	/ˈsəːkl/	n. & v.	圈出	12B
classics	/ˈklæsiks/	n.	杰作	12
classmate	/ˈklɑːsmeit/	n.	同班同学	8
click	/klik/	n. & v.	点击	3B
cliff	/klif/	n.	悬崖	6B
climate	/ˈklaimit/	n.	气候	4A
climb	/klaim/	n. & v.	爬	6B
coast	/kəust/	n. & v.	海岸	9A
coastline	/ˈkəustlain/	n.	海岸线	4A
collect	/kəˈlekt/	v. adj. & adv.	收集	10A
collection	/kəˈlekʃən/	n.	收藏	12
colonization	/ˌkɔlənaiˈzeiʃən/	n.	殖民	9A
comfortable	/ˈkʌmfətəbl/	adj.	舒适的	3B
communication	/kəˌmjuːniˈkeiʃn/	n.	通讯	3
community	/kəˈmjuːniti/	n.	团体，社会	1A
complicate	/ˈkɔmplikeit/	v.	（使）变复杂	12B
conclusion	/kənˈkluːʒən/	n.	结论	8B
congratulate	/kənˈɡrætjuleit/	v.	祝贺	6A
connect	/kəˈnekt/	v.	连接	3
conservation	/ˌkɔnsə(ː)ˈveiʃən/	n.	保存	2B
constantly	/ˈkɔnstəntli/	adv.	持续地	6B
consultant	/kənˈsʌltənt/	n.	顾问	3
consume	/kənˈsjuːm/	v.	消费	11
container	/kənˈteinə/	n.	容器	11
context clues			上下文线索	8B
continue	/kənˈtinjuː/	v.	继续	2B
conventional	/kənˈvenʃənl/	adj.	常规的	11B
counter	/ˈkauntə/	n. adv. & prep.	计算器，柜台	9
cover	/ˈkʌvə/	n. & v.	封面，覆盖	1B
crash	/kræʃ/	n. & v.	碰撞	10B
create	/kriˈeit/	v.	创造	9A
crisis	/ˈkraisis/	n.	危机	2
crossword	/ˈkrɔswəːd/	n.	纵横字谜	3B
crowded	/ˈkraudid/	adj.	拥挤的	7
crucial	/ˈkruːʃiəl/	adj.	至关紧要的	3A
current	/ˈkʌrənt/	adj.	当前的	11B

D

danger	/ˈdeindʒə/	n.	危险	2B
dangerous	/ˈdeindʒrəs/	adj.	危险的	6B
dash	/dæʃ/	n. & v.	短跑，赛跑	6
december	/diˈsembə/	n.	十二月	10A
defense	/diˈfens/	n. & v.	防卫	3
deforestation	/diˌfɔrisˈteiʃən/	n.	采伐森林	9A
degree	/diˈgriː/	n.	度，学位，地位	1A
demand	/diˈmɑːnd/	n. & v.	要求	1A
department	/diˈpɑːtmənt/	n.	部，局，处，科	6
depend	/diˈpend/	v.	依靠	5B
desert	/diˈzəːt/	n.	沙漠	4A
destroy	/disˈtrɔi/	v.	破坏	2B
determine	/diˈtəːmin/	v.	决定	1B
dioxide	/daiˈɔksaid/	n.	二氧化物	2
dirty	/ˈdəːti/	v. & adj.	弄脏，脏的	2A
discover	/disˈkʌvə/	v.	发现	8B
discussion	/disˈkʌʃən/	n.	讨论	12A
disease	/diˈziːz/	n.	疾病	2A
dismiss	/disˈmis/	v.	解散，开除	1
dispose	/disˈpəuz/	v.	处置；处理	11
dollar	/ˈdɔlə/	n.	美元	10
drain	/drein/	n.	排水沟	11B
dramatic	/drəˈmætik/	adj.	戏剧性的	4A
draw	/drɔː/	n. & v.	拉	9A
drop	/drɔp/	n. & v.	滴，落下	7B

E

economically	/iːkəˈnɔmikəli/	adv.	经济地	12B
education	/ˌedju(ː)ˈkeiʃən/	n.	教育	1A
efficient	/iˈfiʃənt/	adj.	有效率的	9
effort	/ˈefət/	n.	努力	11A
Egypt	/ˈiːdʒipt/	n.	埃及	11A
elastic	/iˈlæstik/	adj.	弹性的	6B
electrical	/iˈlektrik(ə)l/	adj.	电力的	1A
electricity	/ilekˈtrisiti/	n.	电流	11B
else	/els/	adj. & adv.	其他的	1B
embarrass	/imˈbærəs/	v.	使困窘	10B

empty	/'empti/	v. & adj.	空的	11A
encourage	/in'kʌridʒ/	v.	鼓励	11
enforce	/in'fɔːs/	v.	强制执行	11B
enrich	/in'ritʃ/	vt.	使丰富	1A
enrollment	/in'rəulmənt/	n.	注册	1A
enter	/'entə/	n. & v.	进入	8
entrance	/'entrəns/	n.	入口	2A
environment	/in'vaiərənmənt/	n.	环境	6B
essay	/'esei/	n. & v.	企图，散文	12A
establish	/is'tæbliʃ/	v.	建立	5A
estimate	/'estimeit/	n. & v.	估计	6B
Europe	/'juərəp/	n.	欧洲	2A
European	/ˌjuərə'pi(ː)ən/	n. & adj.	欧洲的，欧洲人	11A
examination	/igˌzæmi'neiʃən/	n.	考试	8
example	/ig'zɑːmpl/	n.	例子	2A
excellent	/'eksələnt/	adj.	卓越的	12
excitement	/ik'saitmənt/	n.	刺激，兴奋	6B
exercise	/'eksəsaiz/	n. & v.	锻炼	6
exhaust	/ig'zɔːst/	v.	用尽	11B
expand	/iks'pænd/	v.	扩张	9A
expensive	/iks'pensiv/	adj.	昂贵的	8A
experiment	/iks'perimənt/	n. & v.	实验	8B
explore	/iks'plɔː/	v.	探险	3B
express	/iks'pres/	n. & v.	表达	1B
extreme	/iks'triːm/	n. & adj.	极端，极端的	4A
extremely	/iks'triːmli/	adv.	极端地	6A

F

favorable	/'feiərəbl/	adj.	赞成的，有利的	1B
feast	/fiːst/	n.	盛宴	5
fight	/fait/	n. & v.	打架，打斗	10A
flood	/flʌd/	n. & v.	洪水，淹没	4B
fond	/fɔnd/	adj.	喜爱的	12
fool	/fuːl/	n. v. & adj.	蠢人；愚蠢的	1B
forecast	/'fɔːkɑːst/	n. & v.	预报	4
forest	/'fɔrist/	n. & adj.	森林	2B
frond	/frɔnd/	n.	叶，植物体	1B
fruitfully	/'fruːtfuli/	adv.	成果丰硕地，富有成效地	12B
future	/'fjuːtʃə/	n. & adj.	未来	2B

G

garbage	/ˈgɑːbidʒ/	n.	垃圾	2
gather	/ˈgæðə/	n. & v.	集合	3A
global	/ˈgləubəl/	adj.	球形的，全世界的	3A
glossary	/ˈglɔsəri/	n.	术语表；词汇表	8B
glove	/glʌv/	n. & v.	手套	11A
glow	/gləu/	v.	发光，发热	7B
gold	/gəuld/	n. & adj.	黄金，金的	6A
government	/ˈgʌvənmənt/	n.	政府	2B
grand	/grænd/	adj.	盛大的，主要的	7B
grateful	/ˈgreitful/	adj.	感激的	9
greet	/griːt/	v.	问候	7B
grin	/grin/	n. & v.	露齿笑	12A
grow	/grəu/	v.	成长	7A
guess	/ges/	n. & v.	猜测	7A
guide	/gaid/	n. & v.	向导，引导	3B

H

hacker	/ˈhækə/	n.	电脑黑客	3
harm	/hɑːm/	n. & v.	伤害	2
harvest	/ˈhɑːvist/	n. & v.	收获	5
Hawaii	/hɑːˈwaiiː/	n.	夏威夷	7B
hide	/haid/	n. & v.	掩藏，躲藏	7B
hit	/hit/	n. & v.	打击	6B
holiday	/ˈhɔlədi/	n.	假日	5B
honour	/ˈɔnə/	n. & v.	荣誉；尊敬	5A
hopeless	/ˈhəuplis/	adj.	没有希望的	6
huge	/hjuːdʒ/	adj.	巨大的	4B
hunt	/hʌnt/	n. & v.	打猎，搜索	6B
hurricane	/ˈhʌrikən/	n.	飓风	4B

I

imagine	/iˈmædʒin/	v.	想象	12
immediate	/iˈmiːdjət/	adj.	紧接的	6B
impress	/imˈpres/	v.	印象	9
impression	/imˈpreʃən/	n.	印象	1B
improve	/imˈpruːv/	v.	改善	9A
include	/inˈkluːd/	v.	包含	5B

incredibly	/inˈkredəbli/	adv.	不可置信地	7
index	/ˈindeks/	n. & v.	索引	12B
indicate	/ˈindikeit/	v.	指出	12B
indigenous	/inˈdidʒinəs/	adj.	本土的	9A
information	/ˌinfəˈmeiʃən/	n.	信息	8A
initially	/iˈniʃəli/	adv.	最初地	9A
ink	/iŋk/	n.	墨水	11A
innocently	/ˈinəsntli/	adv.	无辜地	10B
integrate	/ˈintigreit/	v.	结合	9A
intelligence	/inˈtelidʒəns/	n.	智力	1B
intelligently	/inˈtelidʒəntli/	adv.	聪明地	12B
Internet	/ˈintənet/	n.	因特网	3A
intimate	/ˈintimit/	adj.	亲密的	5A
introduction	/ˌintrəˈdʌkʃən/	n.	介绍	8
involve	/inˈvɔlv/	v.	包括；涉及	6B
island	/ˈailənd/	n. & v.	岛	7B

J

jeopardize	/ˈdʒepədaiz/	v.	危害	11B
jog	/dʒɔg/	n. & v.	慢跑	6
judge	/dʒʌdʒ/	n. & v.	判断	1B

K

kid	/kid/	n.	小孩	10A
kill	/kil/	v.	杀死	2A
knowledge	/ˈnɔlidʒ/	n.	知识	1A

L

lamp	/læmp/	n. & v.	灯	7A
lecture	/ˈlektʃə/	n. & v.	演讲	1
leftover	/leftˈəuvə/	n. & adj.	剩余物	11A
leisurely	/ˈleʒəli/	adv.	从容不迫	7B
lightly	/ˈlaitli/	adv.	轻轻地	12A
limit	/ˈlimit/	n. & v.	限制	3B
link	/liŋk/	n. & v.	连接	3B
lonely	/ˈləunli/	adj.	孤独的	7
long-jump			跳远	6A
Los Angeles		n.	洛杉矶	4A

M

magazine	/ˌmægəˈziːn/	n.	杂志	9
magic	/ˈmædʒik/	n. & adj.	魔法，有魔力的	7B
mail	/meil/	n. & v.	邮件	10
major	/ˈmeidʒə/	n. v. & adj.	主修	1
mark	/mɑːk/	n. & v.	标记	12B
mask	/mɑːsk/	n.	面具	2
mathematics	/ˌmæθiˈmætiks/	n.	数学	1
measure distance			测量距离	4A
Mediterranean	/ˌmeditəˈreinjən/	n. & adj.	地中海	2A
menu	/ˈmenjuː/	n.	菜单	3B
message	/ˈmesidʒ/	n.	消息	8
mind	/maind/	n. & v.	意见，注意	8B
misread	/misˈriːd/	v.	读错	8B
mistake	/misˈteik/	n. & v.	错误；犯错，弄错	1B
modem	/ˈməudəm/	n.	调制解调器	3
modern	/ˈmɔdən/	adj.	现代的	2B
moment	/ˈməumənt/	n.	片刻	10B
money	/ˈmʌni/	n.	钱	2B
muscle	/ˈmʌsl/	n.	肌肉	6

N

narrow	/ˈnærəu/	n. & v.	窄的	2A
nation	/ˈneiʃən/	n.	国家	2B
national	/ˈnæʃənəl/	adj.	国家的	5A
nationality	/ˌnæʃəˈnæliti/	n.	国籍	12
natural	/ˈnætʃərəl/	adj.	自然的	11
nature	/ˈneitʃə/	n.	自然	2B
necessary	/ˈnesisəri/	n. & adj.	必需品，必需的	2B
network	/ˈnetwəːk/	n.	网络	3
nod	/nɔd/	n. & v.	点头	12A
nuclear power		n.	核动力	11B

O

objective	/əbˈdʒektiv/	n.	目标	9A
obligation	/ˌɔbliˈgeiʃən/	n.	义务	5A
observance	/əbˈzəːvəns/	n.	遵守	5A

occasion	/əˈkeiʒən/	n.	场合，时机	5A
occur	/əˈkəː/	v.	发生	5B
official	/əˈfiʃəl/	n. & adj.	官员，官方的	5A
online	/ɔnˈlain/	n.	联机	3A
opera	/ˈɔpərə/	n.	歌剧	3A
original	/əˈridʒənəl/	adj.	原始的，最初的	7B
ounce	/auns/	n.	盎司	10
overall length			全长	9A
overestimate	/ˌəuvəˈestimeit/	n. & v.	评价过高	1B

P

Pacific Ocean		n.	太平洋	7B
packet	/ˈpækit/	n. & v.	包装	10B
palm	/pɑːm/	n. & v.	棕榈；手掌	4A
participate local			本地参与	3A
passenger	/ˈpæsindʒə/	n.	乘客	9
percent	/pəˈsent/	n.	百分比	5
perfect	/ˈpəːfikt/	n. v. & adj.	完美的	7B
personally	/ˈpəːsənəli/	adv.	亲自	6A
phrase	/freiz/	n. & v.	短语	12B
piano	/piˈɑːnəu/	n.	钢琴	10A
pilot	/ˈpailət/	n. & v.	飞行员，驾驶	4B
plant	/plɑːnt/	n. & v.	植物，种植	2B
pluming	/plʌmiŋ/	n.	（建筑物的）管路系统，自来水管道	1A
polar region			极地地区	9A
political	/pəˈlitikəl/	adj.	政治的	3A
pollution	/pəˈluːʃen/	n.	污染	2
popular	/ˈpɔpjulə/	adj.	流行的	8A
pore	/pɔː/	v.	熟读	12
portfolio	/pɔːtˈfəuljəu/	n.	投资组合，有价证券组合	3A
position	/pəˈziʃən/	n. & v.	位置，安置	5B
postman	/ˈpəustmən/	n.	邮差	10
pour	/pɔː/	v.	倾泻	2A
practice	/ˈpræktis/	n.	练习	10A
predict	/priˈdikt/	v.	预知	9A
prepare	/priˈpɛə/	v.	准备	5
president	/ˈprezidənt/	n.	总统，校长	5A
problem	/ˈprɔbləm/	n.	问题	2A

proclaim	/prə'kleim/	v.	宣布，声明	5A
profession	/prə'feʃən/	n.	职业，专业	1A
professor	/prə'fesə/	n.	教授	12
project	/'prɔdʒekt/	n. & v.	计划	9A
promote	/prə'məut/	v.	促进	9A
propose	/prə'pəuz/	v.	计划，建议	5A
psychologist	/sai'kɔlədʒist/	n.	心理学者	6B
pumpkin	/'pʌmpkin/	n.	南瓜	5
puzzle	/'pʌzl/	n. & v.	迷惑	3B

Q

| quarter | /'kwɔ:tə/ | n. | 四分之一 | 2A |

R

radiant	/'reidjənt/	adj.	发光的	12A
railway	/'reilwei/	n.	铁路	7A
rainstorm	/rein'stɔ:m/	n.	暴风雨	4
rapidly	/'ræpidli/	adv.	迅速地	1A
rashness	/'ræʃnis/	n.	轻率	12A
react	/ri'ækt/	vi.	起反应	1B
realize	/'riəlaiz/	v.	认识到	9B
recognize	/'rekəgnaiz/	v.	承认；认为	5A
recommend	/rekə'mend/	v.	推荐	5A
recommendation	/ˌrekəmen'deiʃən/	n.	推荐	3B
record	/'rekɔ:d/	n. & v.	报告，记录	2B
recycle	/ˌri:'saikl/	n. & v.	再循环	11A
relation	/ri'leiʃən/	n.	关系	5A
relaxation	/ˌri:læk'seiʃən/	n.	放松	12
relay	/'ri:lei/	n. & v.	接力赛	6A
remain	/ri'mein/	v.	保持	2B
requirement	/ri'kwaiəmənt/	n.	需求	3
research	/ri'sə:tʃ/	n. & v.	研究	3A
reservation	/ˌrezə'veiʃən/	n.	保留	3A
resort	/ri'zɔ:t/	n. & v.	旅游胜地，度假胜地	4A
resource	/ri'sɔ:s/	n.	资源	11B
response	/ris'pɔns/	n.	回答；回应	5A
restaurant	/'restərɔnt/	n.	餐馆	5
reunion	/ri:'ju:njən/	n.	团圆	3A
reuse	/'ri:'ju:z/	n. & v.	再使用；再利用	11

reuse material		n.	再生资源	11A
risky	/ˈriski/	adj.	危险的	6B
roar	/rɔː/	n. & v.	吼叫；咆哮	4B
rock	/rɔk/	n. & v.	岩石；摇动	2A
rubbish	/ˈrʌbiʃ/	n.	垃圾	11A
rule	/ruːl/	n. & v.	规则	8B

S

safe	/seif/	n. & adj.	安全，安全的	2A
sake	/seik/	n.	缘故	12B
San Francisco		n.	旧金山	4A
sand	/sænd/	n. & v.	沙子	4A
satellite	/ˈsætəlait/	n.	人造卫星	4B
scatter	/ˈskætə/	v.	分散	9A
scene	/siːn/	n.	场面，情景	7B
scholarship	/ˈskɔləʃip/	n.	奖学金	6A
scientist	/ˈsaiəntist/	n.	科学家	8A
score	/skɔː/	n. & v.	计分；得分	1B
scroll	/skrəul/	n. & v.	滚屏；滚动	3B
search	/səːtʃ/	n. & v.	搜寻	8
second	/ˈsekənd/	n. v. & adj.	第二	6
security	/siˈkjuəriti/	n.	安全	3
seek	/siːk/	v.	寻找	6B
semester	/siˈmestə/	n.	学期	1
send	/send/	v.	送，寄	8A
separate	/ˈsepəreit/	adj. & v.	分开的	4A
separately	/ˈsepərətli/	adv.	个别地；分开地	11A
sequence	/ˈsiːkwəns/	n.	次序	12B
settler	/ˈsetlə/	n.	移民者	5
sewage-treatment			污水处理	2
shake	/ʃeik/	n. & v.	摇动	12A
shine	/ʃain/	n. & v.	光亮，发光	1B
shortage	/ˈʃɔːtidʒ/	n.	短缺，匮乏	11B
similar	/ˈsimilə/	adj.	相似的	3A
single	/ˈsiŋgl/	n. v. & adj.	单一的	11A
single	/siŋgl/	n. & v.	个别的；一对一的；真诚的	12B
situation	/ˌsitjuˈeiʃən/	n.	情形	1B
skyscraper	/ˈskaiskreipə/	n.	摩天大楼	7B
slurp	/sləːp/	n.	喷喷吃的声音	5

snap	/snæp/	n. v. & adj.	（使）断裂；绷断	4B
sneaker	/'sni:kə/	n.	运动鞋	6
society	/sə'saiəti/	n.	社会	6B
software	/'sɔftwɛə/	n.	软件	8A
solar	/'səulə/	adj.	日光的	11B
speechless	/'spi:tʃlis/	adj.	不能说话的	1B
spring	/spriŋ/	n. & v.	春天；温泉	4A
square	/skwɛə/	n. v. & adj.	（用于数字的表示面积）平方	2A
stadium	/'steidiəm/	n.	露天大型运动场	6A
stamp	/stæmp/	n. & v.	邮票，踩（脚）	10A
stock	/stɔk/	n.	股票	3A
stream	/stri:m/	n. & v.	溪，流	2
structure	/'strʌktʃə/	n. & v.	结构，建筑	8B
stupid	/'stju:pid/	adj.	愚蠢的	1B
subject	/'sʌbdʒikt/	n.	科目	8
subway	/'sʌbwei/	n.	地铁	9
successfully	/sək'sesfuli/	adv.	成功地	8B
succession	/sək'seʃən/	n.	连续	4
sulfur	/'sʌlfə/	n. & v.	硫磺	2
sunny	/'sʌni/	adj.	阳光充足的	4
sunshine	/'sʌnʃain/	n.	阳光	4
supermarket	/'sju:pə,mɑ:kit/	n.	超级市场	10B
surely	/'ʃuəli/	adv.	的确地	8B
surfing	/'sə:fiŋ/	n.	网络冲浪	3A
surprise	/sə'praiz/	n. v. & adj.	惊奇	8A
survival	/sə'vaivəl/	n.	幸存	11B
system	/'sistəm/	n.	系统	8A

T

technique	/tek'ni:k/	n.	技术	11A
technology	/tek'nɔlədʒi/	n.	科技，技术	1A
term	/tə:m/	n.	学期	3A
theatre	/'θiətə/	n.	剧场	7A
threat	/θret/	n.	威胁	6B
thrill	/θril/	n.	兴奋感，激动，震撼	6B
thunder	/'θʌndə/	n. & v.	雷，打雷	4B
tie up			绑好，占用，合伙	12B
tip	/tip/	n. & v.	小费；给小费	5
title	/'taitl/	n. v. & adj.	标题	8B

tolerant	/'tɔlərənt/	adj.	容忍的	12A
track	/træk/	n. & v.	（赛场的）跑道	6A
tracksuit	/'træksuit/	n. & v.	运动服	6
traffic	/'træfik/	n. & v.	交通	9
tributary	/'tribjutəri/	n.	（流入大河或湖泊的）支流	9A
tropical	/'trɔpikl/	adj.	热带的	7B
turkey	/'tə:ki/	n.	火鸡	5
type	/taip/	n. & v.	类型，打字	5B

U

unbelievable	/ˌʌnbi'li:vəbl/	adj.	难以置信的	9
unchecked	/ˌʌn'tʃekt/	adj.	未受制止的	11B
underground	/ˌʌndəgraund/	n. & adj.	地铁，地下的	2
united	/ju'naitid/	adj.	联合的	2B
unusual	/ʌn'ju:ʒuəl/	adj.	不平常的	1B
utilize	/ju:'tilaiz/	v.	利用	11B

V

vacation	/və'keiʃən/	n. & v.	假期	5B
various	/'vɛəriəs/	adj.	各种各样的	1A
vast	/va:st/	adj.	巨大的	12A
vendor	/'vendɔ:/	n.	卖主	3A
vernacular	/və'nækjulə/	adj.	本国的	12A
vertical margin			（绳）垂直缘	12B
vest	/vest/	n. & v.	汗衫	12A
virtual	/'və:tjuəl/	adj.	模拟的，虚拟的	3A
voice	/vɔis/	n. & v.	声音	9B
volunteer	/ˌvɔlən'tiə/	n. v. & adj.	志愿者，志愿的	12A

W

waste	/weist/	n. v. & adj.	废物	2A
wasteful	/'weistful/	adj.	浪费的	11B
weather	/'weðə/	n. v. & adj.	天气	4
website	/web'sait/	n.	网站，网址	8
weekend	/wi:k'end/	n. v. & adj.	周末	7
weigh	/wei/	v.	重	10
west	/west/	n. adj. & adv.	西方	12A
whereas	/wɛər'æz/	conj.	然而	12A

whiz	/hwiz/	n. & v.	能手；善于…的人	3B
wisdom	/ˈwizdəm/	n.	智慧	12A
wonder	/ˈwʌndə/	n. v. & adj.	惊奇	3
wonderful	/ˈwʌndəful/	adj.	极好的	7
wooden	/ˈwudn/	adj.	木制的	9B
World Wide Web			万维网	3A
worth	/wə:θ/	adj.	有…价值，值…钱	7

Y

| yoga | /ˈjəugə/ | n. | 瑜伽 | 7 |

试卷说明：

　　本试卷分试卷一（选择题）和试卷二（非选择题）两部分，共五道大题。其中 part I～part IV 为试卷一； part V 为试卷二。共 100 分。考试时间 120 分钟。

Model Test 1

试　卷　一

注意事项：

　　1. 答试卷一前，考生务必将自己的姓名、准考证号、科目代号（英语）、试卷类型（A）用 2B 的铅笔填写在答题卡上。

　　2. 每小题选出答案后，用铅笔把答题卡上对应题目的答案标号涂黑。不能答在试卷上。

　　3. 考试结束后，考生将本试卷和答题卡以并交回。

Part I　阅读理解（本题共 30 分，每小题 2 分）

　　阅读下列短文，并做每篇后面的题目。从四个选项中，选出能回答所提问题或完成所给的句子的答案，并把答案涂在答题卡的相应位置上。

(1)

　　Samuel Langhorne Clemens grew up in a small town beside the Mississippi river around the middle of the nineteenth century. He liked to watch the steamboats traveling along the river. When he was seventeen, he went east to New York, but he never forgot his boyhood experiences. At the age of twenty-one he returned home and became a steamboat pilot. He was very happy on the river.

　　Later, when he began to write stories, he used the name Mark Twain, which was a term used by riverboat men. Most people forgot that his really name was Samuel Clemens.

　　Mark Twain wrote many famous stories, but he is remembered most for his stories about boys. He knew how young people felt about living in a world controlled by adults.

　　One of his best stories tells us about Tom Sawyer, an ordinary American boy who kept getting into trouble. Almost everyone knows how Tom gets his aunt Polly's fence painted.

　　1) Tom Sawyer is a famous _____.

　　　　A. character in one of Mark Twain's stories

　　　　B. writer in American history

　　　　C. steamboat pilot on the Mississippi river

　　　　D. American boy who used the name Mark Twain

　　2) The small town where Samuel Clemens lived is _____ of New York.

　　　　A. In the west　　　　　　　　　　B. to the west

　　　　C. to the south　　　　　　　　　　D. in the east

3) Riverboat men often used the term "mark twain" on the steamboat _____.

    A. When they wanted to read stories

    B. When the river was deep enough for the boat to sail

    C. Because they forgot his real name

    D. Because they wanted to have their fence painted

4) From the story we can learn that Mark Twain is famous for his _____.

    A. childhood experiences   B. stories about the sea

    C. life on the rive   D. books about boys

5) Which of the following is True about Mark Twain?

    A. He once worked as a plane pilot.

    B. He began to write stories when he was over 30.

    C. He stayed in New York for about four years.

    D. He went to New York when he was 21.

(2)

Australia and the United States are about the same in size, and their western lands are both not rich in soil. It was the eastern coast of Australia and America that the English first settled, and both colonies soon began to develop towards the west. However, it was not because the population was increasing that this westward movement took place. It was mainly because the English were searching for better land. Settlements of the western part of both countries developed quickly after gold was discovered in America in 1849 and in Australia two years later.

There are some big differences between these two countries as well. The United States gained its independence from England by revolution while Australia won its independence without having to go to war. Australia, unlike the United States, was firstly turned into a colony by English prisoners and its economic development was in wheat growing and sheep raising. By 1922, for example, Australia had fifteen times more sheep than it had people, or almost half as many sheep as there are people today in the United States. Yet, in spite of these and other main differences, Australia and the United States have more in common with each other than either one has with most of the rest of the world.

6) In the early history of America and Australia, both colonies developed towards the west firstly for the reason that _____.

    A. The population was increasing rapidly in the east

    B. The English thought there might be richer land there

    C. Gold was discovered there

    D. Fewer people lived there

7) In the early 1920s, _____.

    A. Australia had one fifteenth as many people as sheep

    B. There were more sheep in Australia than in the united States

    C. The population in Australia was greater than that of the United States

    D. The United States had twice as many sheep as people

8) Gold was discovered in Australia in _____.

    A. 1849   B. 1847

    C. 1840   D. 1851

9) Australia, unlike the United States, _____.

    A. did not discover gold until the late 1840s

    B. was the last and biggest continent to be discovered

    C. was not rich in gold in its western part

    D. won its independence by peaceful means

10) The last sentence in the last paragraph " …Australia and the United States have more in common with each other than either one has with most of the rest of the world" means _____.

    A. the United States and Australia do not have any main differences

    B. the United States and Australia have nothing in common with the rest of the world

    C. the United States and Australia have much more in common than they have with other countries

    D. the United States and Australia have a lot of differences although they share something in common

(3)

The office has always been a place to get ahead. Unfortunately, it is also a place where a lot of natural resources start to fall behind. Take a look around next time you're at work. See how many lights are left on when people leave.

See how much paper is being wasted. How much electricity is being used to run computers that are left on. Look at how much water is being wasted in the restrooms. And how much solid waste is being thrown out in the rubbish cans. We bet it's a lot.

Now, here are some simple ways you can produce less waste at work. When you are at the copier, only make the copies you need. Use both sides of the paper when writing something less important. Turn off your lights when you leave. Use a lower watt bulb in your lamp. Drink your coffee or tea out of your mugs instead of single-use cups. Set up a recycling box for cans and one for bottles. And when you're in the bathroom brushing your teeth or washing your face, don't let the tap run. Remember, if we use fewer resources today, we'll save more for tomorrow.

11) The main purpose of the passage is to tell people _____.

    A. the disadvantages of working in an office

    B. the waste produced in an office

    C. to save resources when working in an office

    D. how to save water in a restroom

12) How many kinds of waste are mentioned in the passage?

    A. Two.   B. Three.

    C. Four.   D. Five.

13) From the passage we can infer that in the office _____.

    A. using computers is a waste of resource

    B. many people don't turn off the computers after using them

    C. computers are run by electricity

    D. a computer is not a must for working

14) It is suggested that we use both sides of the paper at the copier because _____.

    A. we are short of paper   B. the printing is not important

    C. we should save paper   D. we have to pay for the paper

15) The underlined word "mugs" is most likely to be _____.

    A. a machine that makes coffee

    B. a container that can be used again and again

    C. a paper product for tea

    D. something that can only be found in an office

Part II   词汇与语法结构（本题共 **30** 分，每小题 **1** 分）

    从 A、B、C、D 四个选项中，选出最佳答案涂在答题卡的相应位置上。

16) Why do you represent the matter _____?

    A. in this way   B. in a way

    C. in that way   D. by the way

17) The crisis put his courage and _____ to the test.

    A. receive   B. received

    C. receiving   D. recited

18) Repairing cars is a _____ work.

    A. dirt   B. dirty   C. diet   D. diets

19) Please _____ the window as I can hardly see out.

    A. cleaned   B. cleaning   C. clear   D. clean

20) Their house is _____ ours, but ours has a bigger garden.

    A. similar to   B. similar in   C. similar at   D. similar on

21) The company is casting its net wide in its _____ a new sales director.

    A. research for   B. research of   C. search for   D. search of

22) He talked about how much we owed to our parents, our duty to our country and _____.

    A. so do   B. so on   C. do so   D. do on

23) The government has promised to take _____ to help the unemployed.

    A. measures   B. measure   C. some measure   D. measuring

24) _____ you drive carefully, you will be very safe.

    A. So long as   B. As long as   C. As far as   D. So far as

25) The fish _____ at the bait.

    A. snaped   B. snapped   C. snap   D. snapping

26) Hang the clothes on the _____.

    A. lone   B. lined   C. lining   D. line

27) He should listen to his _____ feelings.

    A. intimate   B. intimating   C. intimates   D. intimated

28) Can you _____ her from this picture?

    A. recognizes   B. recognize   C. recognizing   D. recognized

29) That plane crash _____ only minutes after take-off.

    A. occurred   B. occur   C. occurring   D. occurs

30) She was _____ with health.

    A. radiant   B. gradient   C. radiate   D. radiating

31) He left _____ with my secretary that he would call again. He said that the newcomer is a man of few _____.

    A. words; words   B. word; word

    C. the word; word   D. word; words

32) It's bad _____ to speak with your mouth full of food.

    A. manner   B. manners   C. way   D. thing

33) Every means _____ prevent the water from _____.

    A. are used to; polluting   B. get used to; polluting

    C. is used to; polluted   D. is used to; being polluted

34) These books, which you can get at any bookshops, will give you _____ you need.

    A. all of information   B. all of the informations

    C. all the informations   D. all the information

35) This research has attracted wide _____ coverage and has featured on BBC television's Tomorrow's World.

    A. media   B. information   C. data   D. message

36) Two _____ teachers and four _____ students were praised at the meeting yesterday.

    A. women; girl   B. woman; girl

    C. woman; girls   D. women; girls

37) If you don't take away all your things from the desk, there won't be enough _____ for my stationery.

    A. area   B. place   C. room   D. surface

38) After the battle they buried _____ and brought with _____.

    A. the death, the wounded   B. the deadly, the wounded

    C. the died, the wounding   D. the dead, the wounded

39) Now I am on _____ diet. I'm trying to lose _____ weight.

    A. a; /   B. the; /   C. /; the   D. a; a

40) In our spare time, my little sister enjoys playing _____ violin, while I like playing _____ football.

    A. the; the   B. /; the   C. the; /   D. /; /

41) I'd rather ride a bike as bike riding has _____ of the trouble of taking buses.

    A. much   B. all   C. either   D. none

42) There are six engineers in our team. _____ are from Japan.

    A. The six of them   B. Six of them

    C. Six they   D. All six

43) —What date will tomorrow be?

    —It will be _____.

    A. a fine day   B. April the sixth

    C. Saturday   D. April six

44) 6 _____ 3 is two.

    A. divides by   B. divided by

    C. is divided by   D. divided into

45) The map is _____ small as that one.

    A. half as   B. as half   C. two-ninth as   D. two as

Part III 改错（本题共 10 分，每小题 1 分）

从 A、B、C、D 四个选项中，选出答案涂在答题卡相应的位置上。

46) The girls <u>were sorry</u> (A) <u>to had missed</u> (B) the singers <u>when</u> (C) they <u>arrived at</u> (D) the airport.

47) Mary <u>and</u> (A) her sister <u>studied</u> (B) biology <u>last year</u> (C), and so <u>does Jean</u> (D).

48) A book of many pages <u>would be needed</u> (A) <u>to just list</u> (B) <u>all the</u> (C) animals <u>native</u> (D) to South America.

49) The reason for my <u>return</u> (A) <u>is</u> (B) <u>because</u> (C) I forgot my <u>keys</u> (D).

50) He <u>knows</u> (A) to repair <u>the</u> (B) carburetor without <u>taking</u> (C) the whole car <u>apart</u> (D).

51) The government <u>is believed to be</u> (A) considering <u>to pass</u> (B) a law <u>making</u> (C) it a crime <u>to import</u> (D) any kind of weapon.

52) <u>While</u> (A) the two reappeared after <u>being absent</u> (B) for over a month, everyone in the expedition was surprised to find <u>them</u> (C) <u>so little changed</u> (D).

53) Dr. Edwards has <u>repeatedly</u> (A) advised Henry to stop <u>to smoke</u> (B), if he <u>hopes to stay</u> (C) <u>in</u> (D) good health.

54) <u>Among</u> (A) the most remarkable eyes are <u>those of</u> (B) the dragonfly, <u>for this insect</u> (C)

has compound eyes <u>make up</u> (D) of tiny eyes.

55) <u>Having ate</u> (A) lunch, the three boys <u>got on</u> (B) their bikes and <u>began a 50-mile</u> (C) trip through the <u>foothills</u> (D).

Part IV　完形填空（本题共 **10** 分，每小题 **0.5** 分）

阅读下列短文，掌握其大意。选出一个最佳答案，并把答案画在答题纸的相应位置上。

The measure of a man's real character is what he would do if he knew he would never be found out.

Thomas Macaulay. Some thirty years ago, I was studying in a public school in New York. One day, Mrs. O'Neil gave a math ___56___ to our class. When the papers were ___57___ she discovered that twelve boys had make exactly the ___58___ mistakes throughout the test.

This is nothing really new about ___59___ in exams. Perhaps that was why Mrs. O'Neil ___60___ even say a word about it. She only asked the twelve boys to ___61___ after class. I was one of the twelve.

Mrs. O'Neil asked ___62___ questions, and she didn't ___63___ us either. Instead, she wrote on the blackboard the ___64___ words by Thomas Macaulay. She often ordered us to ___65___ these words into our exercise books one hundred times.

I don't know about other eleven boys. Speaking for myself I can say: it was the most important single ___66___ of my life. Thirty years after being introduced to Macaulay's words, they ___67___ seem to me the best yardstick, because they give us a ___68___ to measure ourselves rather than others.

___69___ of us are asked to make great decisions about nations going to war or armies going to battle. But all of us are called ___70___ daily to make a great many personal decisions should the wallet, found in the street, be put into a pocket ___71___ turned over to the policeman? Should the ___72___ change received at the store be forgotten or ___73___? Nobody will know except ___74___. But you have to live with yourself, and it is always ___75___ to live with some you respect.

56) A. test　　　　　B. problem　　　　C. paper　　　　　D. lesson

57) A. examined　　　B. completed　　　C. marked　　　　D. answered

58) A. easy　　　　　B. funny　　　　　C. same　　　　　D. serious

59) A. lying　　　　　B. cheating　　　　C. guessing　　　　D. discussing

60) A. didn't　　　　　B. did　　　　　　C. would　　　　　D. wouldn't

61) A. come　　　　　B. leave　　　　　C. remain　　　　　D. apologize

62) A. no　　　　　　B. certain　　　　　C. many　　　　　D. more

63) A. excuse　　　　B. reject　　　　　C. help　　　　　　D. scold

64) A. above　　　　　B. common　　　　C. following　　　　D. unusual

65) A. repeat　　　　　B. get　　　　　　C. put　　　　　　D. copy

66) A. chance　　　　B. incident　　　　C. lesson　　　　　D. memory

67) A. even　　　　　B. still　　　　　　C. always　　　　　D. almost

68) A. way   B. sentence   C. choice   D. reason
69) A. All   B. Few   C. Some   D. None
70) A. out   B. for   C. up   D. upon
71) A. and   B. or   C. then   D. but
72) A. extra   B. small   C. some   D. necessary
73) A. paid   B. remembered   C. shared   D. returned
74) A. me   B. you   C. us   D. them
75) A. easier   B. more natural   C. better   D. more peaceful

试　卷　二

姓名：　　　　　　　　　　班级：　　　　　　　　　学生证号：

注意事项：

1. 试卷二要用钢笔或圆珠笔将译文直接写在试卷上。
2. 填写清楚姓名、班级及学生证号。

Part V　英汉互译（本题共 20 分，每小题 2 分）

76) Hardly had they arrived at the airport when their teacher told them the good news.

77) It took the students two hours and a half to work out the maths problem.

78) I think it no use crying for his death now.

79) Being /As a Chinese, we should devote ourselves to our motherland.

80) Last week we visited the house where the scientist used to live.

81）她遇到了那个医生。

82）他过去经常在河边散步。

83）自行车有很多优点。

84）她歌唱得好，而且舞跳得也好。

85）我父母一直鼓励我努力学习。

Model Test 2

试 卷 一

注意事项:

1. 答试卷一前，考生务必将自己的姓名、准考证号、科目代号（英语）、试卷类型（A）用 2B 的铅笔填写在答题卡上。

2. 每小题选出答案后，用铅笔把答题卡上对应题目的答案标号涂黑。不能答在试卷上。

3. 考试结束后，考生将本试卷和答题卡以并交回。

Part I　阅读理解（本题共 30 分，每小题 2 分）

阅读下列短文，并做每篇后面的题目。从四个选项中，选出能回答所提问题或完成所给的句子的答案，并把答案涂在答题卡的相应位置上。

(1)

Marco Polo was an Italian traveler who took part in one of the longest land voyages of the Middle Ages. His father and uncle were Venetian businessmen who traveled widely to trade with people in other lands. They even went as far as China, and on their second visit to that country they took young Marco with them. They set out in 1271, crossing Persia, western Asia, and the Gobi desert - places almost unknown to Europeans in those days. they reached Beijing in 1275, where they were welcomed by the Great Mongol conqueror (征服者) Kublai Khan.

In 1292 the three men started on their return journey. It took them three years to reach Venice. They had been away for 24 years and were hardly recognized even by their relatives. At a banquet to celebrate their return, the travelers took out beautiful silks and bags full of jewels. These were the fruits of their trading and gifts from Kublai Khan.

In 1298 Marco Polo was caught in a sea battle between Venice and Genoa. During his captivity (囚禁) he dictated the story of his journeys to a fellow prisoner. It was later published as The Book of Marco Polo and became so popular that it was translated into many languages, and encouraged several later explorers.

1) Marco Polo, together with his father and uncle, traveled a long distance to China.

　　A. Where they had never been before

　　B. For the purpose of trading

　　C. By ship only and without much difficulty

　　D. For adventure and pleasure

2) They stayed in China for ＿＿＿＿ years.

　　A. 17　　　　　　　　B. 4　　　　　　　　C. 24　　　　　　　　D. 3

3) After the three men went back to Venice, people could hardly recognize them because_____.

　A. they spoke a different language

　B. they were too tired after such a journey

　C. they had changed greatly during many years of absence

　D. they didn't want to let people recognize them

4) According to the passage, _____ at a banquet.

　A. they told people about Europe

　B. they gave people gifts brought back from China

　C. they laid out silks and fruits brought from China

　D. they showed people precious stones and silks

5) The Book of Marco Polo was a book first written _____.

　A. in many languages

　B. by Marco Polo in the battle

　C. as a result of his fellow prisoner's help

　D. right after Marco Polo came back from China

(2)

　　There once lived a king who liked the art of mime very much. He thought he was cleverer than any others. So he declared that anyone who could tell what his mime meant could be rewarded with three bags of gold.

　　Thousands tried, but none succeeded. One day a one-eyed beggar was brought to the palace. The old man was good at playing mime. Sitting at the poor man, the king raised one finger. The old man lifted two. The king showed three fingers. Immediately the old beggar raised his fist. The king gave an orange and the poor beggar showed some crumbs in return, "You've got it!" cried the king. He gave the poor beggar the three bags of gold.

　　Later, the king explained to his officials, "One finger means I am the No.1 in the kingdom. He raised two fingers suggesting that I have a prince. Then I remember the prince has a baby, so I should be united as one. An orange referred to the earth. The crumbs stood for grains."

　　But the beggar began his story this way. "The king raised one finger to say I was blind in one eye, but with two fingers I told him I could see no less than others." The king raised three fingers to say we both had three eyes. "I was hurt, so I lifted my fist with anger."

6) The king in the passage was _____.

　A. very clever　　　　　　　　　　　B. very sure of himself

　C. very easy to be cheated　　　　　　D. kind-hearted

7) The poor man got three bags of gold because _____.

　A. he had only one eye

　B. he was good at playing mime

　C. the king thought he could tell what his mime meant

　D. the king was frightened when the beggar raised his fist

8) Which of the following is True according to the passage?

    A. The king was really cleverer than the other.

    B. The king thought the beggar understood him well.

    C. The Kings art of mime was excellent.

    D. One-eyed men are usually very clever.

9) The poor beggar raised his fist to _____.

    A. Show that he was angry with the king

    B. Suggest the king, the prince and his baby should be united as one

    C. Show that he could see as much as others

    D. Ask for rewards as many as possible

10) As a matter of fact, _____.

    A. The beggar couldn't tell the king's mime

    B. The beggar was cleverer than the king

    C. The king was cleverer than the beggar

    D. Both of them were fools

(3)

Almost every family buys at least one copy of newspaper every day. Some people subscribe to (订阅) as many as two or three different newspapers. But why do people in the world read newspapers?

Five hundred years ago, news of important happenings—battles lost and won, kings or rulers overthrown or killed—took months and even years to travel from one country to another. The news passed by word of mouth and was never accurate. Today we can read in our newspapers of important events that occur in faraway countries on the same day they happen.

Besides supplying news from all over the world, newspapers give us a lot of useful information. There are weather reports, radio, television and film guides, book reviews, stories, and, of course, advertisements. There are all sorts of advertisements. The bigger ones are put in by large companies to bring attention to their products. They pay the newspapers thousands of dollars for the advertising space. But it is worth the money for news of their products goes into almost every home in the country. For those who produce newspapers, advertisements are also very important. Money earned from advertisements makes it possible for them to sell their newspapers at a low price and still make a profit (利润).

Newspapers often have information on gardening, cookery and fashion, as well as a small but very popular section on jokes and cartoons.

11) The habit of reading newspapers is _____ nowadays.

    A. widespread in the world

    B. found among a few families

    C. not popular in the world

    D. uncommon in he world

12) A few hundred years ago news did not _____.

    A. travel fast   B. receive attention

    C. spread to other countries   D. take long to reach other countries

13) In the past, news was _____.

    A. sent by telegraph   B. passed from one person to another

    C. sent by registered letters   D. sent by telephone

14) Newspapers also give us information on _____.

    A. large companies   B. every home

    C. the weather   D. advertising space

15) The section on jokes and cartoons is _____.

    A. read only by children   B. of no value

    C. not helpful   D. read by many

Part II 词汇与语法结构（本题共 **30** 分，每小题 **1** 分）

从 A、B、C、D 四个选项中，选出最佳答案涂在答题卡的相应位置上。

16) He is an _____ -looking young man.

    A. profession   B. professions   C. athletics   D. athletic

17) We will go to the _____ to watch a football match.

    A. stadium   B. stadiums   C. some stadium   D. a stadium

18) The value of imports has _____ sharply in the last year.

    A. climbs   B. climbed   C. climbing   D. climb

19) He came towards me, smiled and _____ his hand.

    A. offered   B. offering   C. offer   D. offers

20) Don't _____ on him.

    A. blames   B. blaming   C. blamed   D. blame

21) A passage was cleared through the crowd like _____.

    A. magician   B. magic's   C. magic   D. magicing

22) The office _____ allows users to share files and software, and to use a central printer.

    A. networks   B. networking   C. network   D. some network

23) The development of modern society depends on _____.

    A. sciences   B. some sciences   C. a science   D. science

24) He was _____ to the position of manager.

    A. promoting   B. promoted   C. promotes   D. promote

25) The people of _____ used to mean the British.

    A. England   B. English   C. Englishness   D. England's

26) His story was so funny that the people present couldn't help _____.

    A. laugh   B. laughed   C. laughing   D. laughs

27) Opportunities _____ this did not come every day.

    A. utilizes   B. utilize   C. utilizing   D. utilized

28) In order to save expenses, please _____ your envelopes.

    A. reuse　　　　　　　B. reusing　　　　　　C. reuses　　　　　D. reused

29) She's very _____ in her views.

    A. conventional　　　　B. convectional　　　　C. conventionally　　D. conventionality

30) His only chance of _____ was a heart transplant.

    A. survived　　　　　　B. survival　　　　　　C. surviving　　　　D. survives

31) He drives much _____ than he did five years ago.

    A. careful

    C. more careful

                      B. carefully

                      D. more carefully

32) John plays football _____, if not better than, David.

    A. as well

    C. so well

                      B. as well as

                      D. so well as

33) She got up _____ miss the train.

    A. so early as to

    C. so early as not to

                      B. so early to

                      D. so early not as to

34) In my opinion, he's _____ the most imaginative of all the contemporary poets.

    A. by far　　　　　　　B. at best　　　　　　C. in all　　　　　D. for all

35) I am not satisfied _____ his conduct.

    A. in　　　　　　　　　B. with　　　　　　　C. at　　　　　　D. for

36) She is tall _____ her age.

    A. in　　　　　　　　　B. with　　　　　　　C. because of　　　D. for

37) People in the north mainly _____ wheat.

    A. depend on　　　　　B. live by　　　　　　C. feed on　　　　D. eat up

38) We hadn't met for 20 years, but I recognized her _____ I saw her.

    A. the moment

    C. the moment when

                      B. for the moment

                      D. at the moment when

39) George applied for the position three times _____ he finally got it.

    A. before　　　　　　　B. until　　　　　　　C. when　　　　　D. after

40) Generally speaking, the harder one works, _____.

    A. the better he gets result

    C. he gets better result

                      B. the better result he gets

                      D. does he get better result

41) With the worldwide oil crisis, the price of oil has been raise _____ 15%.

    A. about　　　　　　　B. with　　　　　　　C. of　　　　　　D. by

42) The house built of stone lasts longer than _____ built of wood.

    A. the one　　　　　　B. one　　　　　　　C. that　　　　　D. its

43) E-mail as well as telephones _____ more and more popular in daily communication.

    A. have become

    C. are becoming

                      B. become

                      D. is becoming

44) _____ the essay a second time, the hidden meaning will become clearer to you.

    A. While reading   B. After reading

    C. Your having reading   D. When you read

45) When the farmer came back from work, his pet dog jumped out _____ the door to welcome him.

    A. from   B. from behind   C. of   D. of behind

Part III 改错（本题共 10 分，每小题 1 分）

从 A、B、C、D 四个选项中，选出答案涂在答题卡相应的位置上。

46) Stuart stopped <u>to write</u> (A) his letter <u>because</u> (B) he had to <u>leave</u> (C) <u>for the hospital</u>(D).

47) He isn't <u>driving</u> (A) <u>to the convention</u> (B) <u>in March</u> (C), and neither <u>they are</u> (D).

48) I sometimes wish that my university <u>is</u> (A) <u>as large as</u> (B) State University because our facilities are <u>more</u> (C) limited <u>than</u> (D) theirs.

49) They <u>are</u> (A) going <u>to have to</u> (B) <u>leave soon</u> (C), and <u>so do</u> (D) we.

50) We all <u>laughed</u> (A) <u>when</u> (B) Helen said she <u>could not</u> (C) remember what day <u>was it</u> (D).

51) <u>The equipment</u> (A) <u>in the office</u> (B) <u>was badly</u> (C) in need of <u>to be</u> (D) repaired.

52) Pardon me <u>but</u> (A) I was <u>wondering</u> (B) if you'd mind helping me <u>getting</u> (C) my car <u>starting</u> (D).

53) We thought <u>wrong</u> (A) <u>that</u> (B) her mother <u>should be left</u> (C) in <u>completely ignorance</u> (D).

54) <u>Electric wires</u> (A) are made <u>from copper</u> (B) or lead <u>is</u> (C) common <u>practice</u> (D).

55) Jerry <u>will not lend</u> (A) you the book because <u>he is fearful</u> (B) <u>if</u> (C) you will forget <u>to return it</u> (D).

Part IV 完形填空（本题共 10 分，每小题 0.5 分）

阅读下列短文，掌握其大意。选出一个最佳答案，并把答案画在答题纸的相应位置上。

"I was going to be late ___56___ the manager wasn't going to be ___57___ . Thank God!" The bus ___58___ round the corner and I got on. At 9:25 I was walking into the ___59___ where I work. "I ___60___ the manager doesn't notice. But no ___61___ luck!"

"Smith!" shouted the manager. "Late again! What's your ___62___ this time?" "I'm afraid the bus was late, Mr. Brown." "___63___ up earlier tomorrow! Anyway, get to ___64___ at the counter. We'll be opening in a few minutes."

My first customer was a pretty girl __65__ a red dress. Behind her was a young man carrying something __66__ with brown paper. __67__ few seconds he looked towards the main entrance. The girl asked about opening a bank account. I gave her the necessary information and she walked out. Turning to my next customer, I was terrified to see a gun sticking out of his coat. Then a loud noise __68__ my ears … __69__ seemed a very long time, I opened my eyes and found myself in bed! __70__ shaking from the memory of this terrible dream, I got dressed and ran out of the house. As __71__, the bus wasn't on time, and I arrived at 9:25.

"Smith!" the manager cried out in a voice like __72__. "Late again! Go and start your work at once!" To my __73__, the first customer was a girl __74__ a red dress and behind her stood a man carrying something wrapped in brown paper. The dream! __75__ that the surprise of my life!

56) A. as	B. but	C. and	D. or
57) A. pleased	B. worried	C. sorry	D. patient
58) A. ran	B. came	C. rode	D. drove
59) A. hotel	B. shop	C. bank	D. restaurant
60) A. believe	B. expect	C. guess	D. hope
61) A. much	B. such	C. more	D. this
62) A. excuse	B. idea	C. reply	D. answer
63) A. Hurry	B. Come	C. Catch	D. Get
64) A. business	B. job	C. place	D. spot
65) A. having on	B. wearing	C. putting on	D. dressing
66) A. hidden	B. rolled	C. filled	D. covered
67) A. A	B. Some	C. Every	D. Each
68) A. took	B. shook	C. filled	D. tore
69) A. It	B. When	C. What	D. Which
70) A. Even	B. Still	C. Just	D. Ever
71) A. usual	B. past	C. such	D. yet
72) A. noise	B. thunder	C. shot	D. shout
73) A. belief	B. surprise	C. dream	D. regret
74) A. of	B. with	C. on	D. in
75) A. Was	B. Is	C. Wasn't	D. Isn't

试　卷　二

姓名:　　　　　　　　　　班级:　　　　　　　学生证号:

注意事项:

　　1. 试卷二要用钢笔或圆珠笔将译文直接写在试卷上。

　　2. 填写清楚姓名、班级及学生证号。

Part V　英汉互译（本题共 20 分，每小题 2 分）

76) Yesterday it took us about two hours to finish that job. Or yesterday we spent about two hours finishing that job.

77) It's important for children to learn English and computer well.

78) He didn't work hard last term, as a result, he failed in his math exam.

79) The students were very interested in what the reporter said.

80) When they got to the cinema, the film had already begun.

81）北京是她游览过的最美丽的城市之一。

82）他们在北京生活了很多年。

83）如果努力我们的愿望一定会实现。

84）老师告诉我们这本小说值得一读。

85）我的朋友问我是否我在工作中有困难。

Answer Keys

Unit 1
Exercise 1:

A: Hi, David. <u>What is your major?</u>

A: <u>I am majoring in English.</u>

A: Yes. <u>I find English is very interesting.</u>

Exercise 2:

dismiss	lecture	canteen	stew	cabbage
beef	wonderful	semester	major	mathematics

Exercise 3: 1)～5) D　D　D　B　A

Exercise 4: 1) enrolled　2) increased　3) in this way　4) demands　5) profession

6) look for　7) career　8) electrical　9) avoid　10) various

11) communication　12) attended　13) degrees　14) skill　15) received

Exercise 5: 1)～5) d　a　b　e　c

Exercise 6:

　　对于那些参与并通过公平考试的学生来说，如果他们因为经济原因无法进入大学是很不公平的。 现在仍有待于找到一条合理而有效解决大学生经济问题的方法。高等教育的费用一直在逐年上涨。这种情况下，来自低收入家庭或农村的学生是不可能上得起大学的。

Exercise 7: 1)～5) A　B　D　D　B

Exercise 8: 1) cover　2) try to　3) intelligence　4) shone　5) situation　6) pretty

7) make mistakes　8) overestimated　9) bound to　10) favorable　11) bottom

12) appearance　13) get to know　14) judgment　15) take your time

Exercise 9: 1)～5) b　d　c　a　e

Exercise 10: 1）close 是动词，作谓语，词义是"关上"。

2）watch 是名词，作不定式 to repair 的宾语，词义是"表"。

3）fast 是形容词，作定语，词义是"快的"。

4）like 是介词，作状语，词义是"像…一样"。

5）quiet 是形容词，作表语，词义是"安静"。

6）work 是名词，作主语，词义是"工作"。

Exercise 11: 1）时间过得很快。

Time 是主语，flies 是谓语，fast 是状语。

2）我急于找个工作。

I 是主语，am 是谓语，in a hurry 是表语，to find a job 是状语。

3）你能让他帮助我吗？

you 是主语，can get 是谓语，him 是宾语，to help me 是宾语补足语。

4）全世界人民都希望和平。

The people 是主语，allover the world 是定语，are hoping for 是谓语，peace 是宾语。

5）他给儿子买了些糖。

He 是主语，bought 是谓语，some sweets 是宾语，for his son 是状语。

6）你最好用英语回答问题。

You 是主语，had better answer 是谓语，the question 是宾语，in English 是状语。

Unit 2

Exercise 1:

B: Yes, I do.

A: Polluted water does harm to everyone.

A: We can reduce the water pollution.

Exercise 2:

crack	pollution	hazard	quality	crisis
garbage	stream	form	sulfur	dioxide

Exercise 3: 1)～5) C　C　B　D　D

Exercise 4: 1) pollution　2) certain　3) dirty　4) narrow　5) entrance　　6) quarters　7) no longer　8) disease　9) at present　　10) waste　11) chemical　12) coast　13) pouring into　14) accident　15) square

Exercise 5: 1)～5) e　a　c　b　d

Exercise 6:

你觉得待在家里你就能保证免受各种各样的户外污染吗？ 你觉得在办公室里正在呼吸的空气会比到外面午餐或下班回家路上的空气更干净、更保险吗？ 即使在受烟雾污染的城市里，待在室内实际上比待在室外对健康更有害。显然，我们无论在家还是在办公室都不保险。

Exercise 7: 1)～5) C　C　C　D　D

Exercise 8: 1) in danger　2) government　3) conserve　4) remained　5) destroyed　6) modern　7) technology　8) continued　9) happened　10) bridge　11) clean　12) kilometers　13) hear　14) singer　15) help

Exercise 9: 1)～5) a　c　d　b　e

Exercise 10: 1) toys　2) daughters-in-law; son-in-law　3) Sunday　4) tea　5) keys

Exercise 11: 1)～5) B　C　D　C　D

Exercise 12: 1) masters of the country　　2) pupils' homework

3) the education of China/China's education　　4) International Women's Day

5) half an hour's talk　　6) at my aunt's

7) yesterday's paper　　8) two daughters of her sister-in-law

Unit 3

Exercise 1:

A: Hello, Li Ming. What is the Internet?

B: <u>In short, the Internet is a network of thousands of computers connected.</u>

B: <u>What can I find on the Internet?</u>

B: <u>Thank you for telling me about that.</u>

Exercise 2:

wonder	network	personal	modem	access
hacker	attract	defense	arrant	security

Exercise 3: 1)～5) C D D B A

Exercise 4: 1) right now   2) term   3) similar to   4) wherever   5) public   6) reunion   7) allow
8) crucial   9) participate in   10) reservation   11) political   12) checked out
13) soap   14) surfing   15) stock

Exercise 5: 1)～5) c a e b d

Exercise 6:

五年以前，世界开始密切注意因特网，但是没人考虑过在线购物。

四年以前，因特网仅仅被视为信息技术产业的一部分，仍然没有什么人会预料因特网将成为带领社会发展的新经济形式。

三年以前，没有谁能想象所有的货物都能通过因特网去销售，人们会相信一切商品都可以通过电子商务进行贸易。

Exercise 7: 1)～5) C B D A C

Exercise 8: 1) comfortable   2) point   3) click   4) mouse   5) chance   6) exploring   7) Internet
8) bookmark   9) guided   10) engine   11) search for   12) mountain   13) crossword
14) so on   15) print out

Exercise 9: 1)～5) c a b e d

Exercise 10: 1) a; The   2) The, the, the   3) an, a   4) the   (5) a, the

Exercise 11: 1)～5) D B A A C   6)～10) B A D B B

Unit 4

Exercise 1:

B: <u>Yes, it is. It's better than yesterday.</u>

B: <u>As long as it doesn't rain.</u>

B: <u>Great!</u>

Exercise 2:

weather	rainstorm	fresh	breeze	shining
calm	cloud	rainy	peace	suffer

Exercise 3: 1)～5) C C A A A

Exercise 4: 1) measures   2) distance   3) separated   4) extreme   5) climate   6) beach
7) decided   8) drive to   9) dramatic   10) keep away   11) coastline   12) get over
13) enough   14) attracted   15) As long as

Exercise 5: 1)～5) d a b e c

Exercise 6:

数千年前古代人民发现，夏季的白天比冬季的长，而夏季的黑夜则比冬季的短。他们通过多少代人辛辛苦苦的观察，确认在北半球十二月二十一日的白天最短，过了那天后，白天就渐渐变长，一直到六月二十一日，那天是一年中的白天最长，黑夜最短的一天。

Exercise 7: 1)～5) B　D　D　C　C

Exercise 8: 1) look for　2) quieted　3) snapped　　4) turned...over　5) flooded　6) satellite
7) asked to　8) pilot　　9) in the sky　10) move around　11) roaring　12) through
13) lightning　14) thunder　15) line

Exercise 9: 1)～5) c　a　e　b　d

Exercise 10: 1)～5) A　B　C　D　A　　　6)～10) C　B　C　D　B

Exercise 11: 1) Where is my book? Your book is not here. This is mine.

2) These are our magazines. Theirs are on the bookshelf.

3) These tall trees were planted by the headmaster himself ten years ago.

4) She often helps me with my maths and I often teach her how to speak English.

5) Our teacher often tells us something about the history of our country.

Unit 5

Exercise 1:

A: <u>Hi, Li Ming</u>!

A: <u>Christmas Day is round the corner</u>.

A: <u>Of course</u>.

Exercise 2:

foreign　　corner　　feast　　special　　harvest
delicious　　attention　　consider　　slurp　　soup

Exercise 3: 1)～5) C　C　B　B　B

Exercise 4: 1) special　2) put forward　3) proposed　4) honour　5) bring up　6) in response to
7) governor　8) proclaimed　9) approve　10) established　11) recommend
12) intimate　13) relations　14) recognize　15) occasion

Exercise 5: 1)～5) b　d　c　a　e

Exercise 6:

圣诞节，12 月 25 日，对于大多数英国孩子来说也许是一年中最高兴的一天。他们高兴的赠送礼物。在圣诞节前夜，英国孩子们经常在场的末端挂上一只长筒袜。早晨，他们玩新玩具，中午饭时，就会有一个圣诞蛋糕，他们的父母经常会在蛋糕里放上一个或两个硬币。然后，有趣的是大家看谁会找到那个硬币。

Exercise 7: 1)～5) C　D　C　C　D

Exercise 8: 1) occurred　2) at least　3) national　4) arranged　5) celebrated　6) major
7) travels　8) include　9) settler　10) business　11) depend on　12) position
13) replaced　14) rather than　15) vacation

Exercise 9: 1)～5) e　a　c　b　d

Exercise 10: 1)～5) C　A　C　B　C　　　6)～10) B　A　B　B　B

Exercise 11: 1) My aunt has two daughters. One is a nurse, the other is an actress.

2) Is there anything more to discuss? No, nothing.

3) It's too hot today. Have another cup of ice beer, please.

4) She doesn't want to buy an ice-box, neither do I. But both of us want to buy washers.

5) I have never watched such a wonderful football match as this.

Unit 6

Exercise 1:

B: <u>Football</u>.

B: <u>Many people in the world like football</u>.

B: <u>Great! Let's go</u>.

Exercise 2:

exercise	sneaker	hopeless	notice	tracksuit
present	build	muscle	jog	campus

Exercise 3: 1)～5) B   D   D   D   D

Exercise 4: 1) born in   2) athletic   3) ability   4) extremely   5) champion   6) excellent
7) scholarship   8) tracks   9) records   10) relay   11)personally   12) congratulated
13) stadium   14) medal   15) hero

Exercise 5: 1)～5) c   a   b   e   d

Exercise 6:

体育运动对我们的身体大有好处。他能强壮身体，抑制肥胖，保持健康和合适的身材。对一天大部分时间做脑力劳动的人来说尤为重要。因为在体格的过程中，它能给人一种有益的练习。

Exercise 7: 1)～5) D   A   C   C   A

Exercise 8: 1) take part in   2) dangerous   3) Adventure   4) climbed   5) unknown   6) boasting
7) Up to   8) estimate   9) jumping   10) threat   11) constantly   12) offered
13) comparatively   14) environment   15) seek

Exercise 9: 1)～5) a   c   d   b   e

Exercise 10: 1)～5) C   B   B   D   B   6)～10) C   C   D   B   B

Exercise 11: 1) The students came into the classroom twos and threes.

2) How much is fifteen divided by three?

3) One third of the teachers in this school are middle-aged.

4) The river is five hundred kilometers long and ten meters deep.

5) This playground is ten times wider than that one.

Unit 7

Exercise 1:

B: <u>Good afternoon, sir</u>.

B: <u>Yes, sir. Come in</u>.

B: <u>No problem</u>.

Exercise 2:

sale	accompany	worth	wonderful	lonely

beautiful   yoga   crowded   weekend   incredibly

Exercise 3: 1)～5) C B B A D

Exercise 4: 1) smoking   2) continued   3) blame   4) building   5) burned   6) die   7) dry

8) fire   9) high   10) kicking   11) south   12) Hundreds of   13) lamps

14) port   15) strong

Exercise 5: 1)～5) d a b e c

Exercise 6:

随着中国经济的发展，银行开始在人们生活中起着越来越重要的作用。银行不再是一个仅能存钱取钱的地方。人们也可以在银行交呼机费、手机费，甚至学费。人们还可以向银行申请信用卡或者申请贷款去购买住房和汽车。银行已经成为中国人日常生活中必不可少的一部分。

Exercise 7: 1)～5) B B C B D

Exercise 8: 1) almost   2) leisurely   3) scene   4) island   5) like   6) glow   7) greets

8) different from   9) dramatic   10) dreams of   11) golden   12) magic

13) in the middle of   14) quickly   15) tropical

Exercise 9: 1)～5) c a e b d

Exercise 10: 1)～5) B C D A D   6)～10) D A B C A

Exercise 11: 1) The house is built of bricks.

2) We've heard about / of that movie, but we haven't seen it yet.

3) Helen is suffering from a headache today.

4) Our telephone was out of order and so I couldn't call you.

5) Is this for / on sale?

Unit 8

Exercise 1:

A: Hi, Peter! <u>What are you doing now</u>?

A: Oh, <u>I don't know how to search on the website</u>.

B: <u>You're welcome</u>.

Exercise 2:

examination   click   website   introduction   enter

grade   classmate   search   message   subject

Exercise 3: 1)～5) C D A D A

Exercise 4: 1) expensive   2) allowed   3) history   4) hospital   5) keep on   6) More and more

7) network   8) on-line   9) sent   10) One of   11) Internet   12) set up

13) software   14) surfing   15) at that time

Exercise 5: 1)～5) b e c a d

Exercise 6:

全世界仍有一亿两千五百万的儿童无法上小学。这其中有三分之二是女童。他们必须长时间地干活，帮助家里维持生计，然而不受教育，是很难摆脱贫困线的。只有提供更多的学校教育、更多的教科书以及增加更多的机会才能打破这个恶性循环。我们的梦想正是要让是世界不再有贫困。

Exercise 7: 1)～5) C   B   C   C   C

Exercise 8: 1) chapter   2) science   3) consider   4) else   5) aroused   6) guide   7) slow

8) while   9) information   10) conclusion   11) rules   12) successfully

13) way   14) in such a way   15) thinking of

Exercise 9: 1)～5) b   d   c   a   e

Exercise 10: 1)～5) C   B   B   C   B   6)～10) C   B   B   A   A

Exercise 11: 1) She seems tired. You should let her have a good rest.

2) Doing exercises makes you happy and healthy.

3) Time is up. The class is over.

4) When I went to see him, he has already gone out.

5) Spring is here, but it is still very cold in Beijing.

Unit 9

Exercise 1:

B: Yes, sir. Please get on the car.

A: How much is it?

B: Here is your change, sir.

Exercise 2:

pretty   expensive   inexpensive   grateful   station

least   rush   platform   board   agency

Exercise 3: 1)～5) C   C   D   D   D

Exercise 4: 1) affect   2) climate   3) raise   4) promoted   5) integrate   6) improve   7) link

8) area   9) critics   10) drew up   11) ecological   12) So far as   13) initially

14) regions   15) level of

Exercise 5: 1)～5) d   a   b   e   c

Exercise 6:

史密斯从窗口望出去，这时他看见一辆卡车和一辆轿车撞在了一起。他跑出去帮忙。卡车里只有一位男士，轿车里只有一位女士，两人都没有受伤，但是轿车被撞坏了。

Exercise 7: 1)～5) B   C   B   A   D

Exercise 8: 1) anything   2) angry   3) measure   4) Never   5) chops   6) proud   7) realize

8) dark   9) finally   10) without   11) automobile   12) call out   13) grown ups

14) for a long time   15) how far

Exercise 9: 1)～5) c   a   b   e   d

Exercise 10: 1)～5) B   C   A   C   D   6)～10) B   D   C   D   D

Exercise 11: 1) English is as important as maths.

2) Wang Dong is two years older than me, but I am a head taller than he.

3) "The World Trade Center" is one of the largest and highest buildings in the world.

4) The more you learn, the greater knowledge you get.

5) This river is wider and deeper than that one.

Unit 10

Exercise 1:

　　A: Excuse me. <u>I'd like to mail this letter.</u>

　　A: <u>How postage</u> is for a local letter?

　　A: <u>Thank you very much</u>.

Exercise 2:

mail	cent	ounce	weigh	express
dollar	postman	course	post	office

Exercise 3: 1)～5) C　C　A　B　C

Exercise 4: 1) a bit　2) teacher　3) small　4) dumb　5) collect　6) stamp　7) watched
　　　　　8) piano　9) hate　10) fight　11) address　12) October　13) England
　　　　　14) far from　15) practice

Exercise 5: 1)～5) c　b　a　d　e

Exercise 6:

　　在 24 小时内，中国的新生儿数量约为 52 056 人，而同一时间内死亡的人数约为 12 960 人。这样每天净增人口 39 096 人。按平均 365 天的日历年计算，这些数值显示现在中国人口每年将增加 1427 万。这意味着，如果目前的人口增长率持续下去的话，在 84 年之后，中国的人口将是现在的两倍。

Exercise 7: 1)～5) B　B　A　B　B

Exercise 8: 1) experience　2) asleep　3) biscuit　4) nice　5) managed　6) laughing
　　　　　7) embarrassed　8) crashes　9) piles　10) display　11) full of　12) moment
　　　　　13) pulled out　14) put …in　15) from the bottom of

Exercise 9: 1)～5) e　a　c　b　d

Exercise 10: 1)～5) C　A　B　A　C

Exercise 11: 1) They watch TV every evening.

　　　　　2) I leave by air and arrive there at six tomorrow afternoon.

　　　　　3) How often do you send an E-mail to your mother?

　　　　　4) Your friend looks very young.

　　　　　5) As soon as he comes back, tell him to give me a call.

Exercise 12:

　　The world we <u>live</u> in <u>is</u> a big, big round ball. It is turning all the time, but you cannot <u>see</u> or <u>feel</u> this turning. There <u>are</u> other worlds, too, but the one we <u>live</u> on is called the earth. It is made of soil and rock, trees and grass, air and water, and all the other things around you.

　　The sun <u>shines</u> on the earth, the rain <u>falls</u> on it, the wind <u>blows</u> over it. The sun <u>shines</u> on you, the rain <u>falls</u> on you, and the wind <u>blows</u> your hat off. You <u>live</u> on the earth, and everything around you <u>is</u> part of it.

Unit 11

Exercise 1:

　　A: Hi, Alisa. <u>Do you know how to protect the water resources</u>?

A: <u>Yes. There are other ways</u>.

B: <u>What are they</u>?

B: <u>That's a good idea</u>!

Exercise 2:

resource   society   material   situation   trend

detail   habit   flea   market   rid

Exercise 3: 1)～5) C   B   C   D   B

Exercise 4: 1) shut down   2) efforts   3) waste   4) rubber   5) However   6) single   7) treats

8) material   9) pollution   10) reuse   11) separately   12) technique   13) used to

14) such as   15) work hard

Exercise 5: 1)～5) e   d   c   b   a

Exercise 6:

新闻报道说世界上的淡水供应正陷入危机。这一警告是二十一世纪世界水问题委员会提出的。该组织的建立就是为了研究世界淡水供应的各种情况。世界淡水供应的问题像影响人类一样影响着野生动植物。在 1998 年，有两千五百万人因供水、污染和其他水问题造成的环境灾害沦为难民。

Exercise 7: 1)～5) C   B   A   C   B

Exercise 8: 1) energy   2) worry   3) resources   4) exhausted   5) mankind   6) solar

7) conventional   8) depend on   9) for example   10) jeopardize   11) shortage

12) slowed down   13) survival   14) Sooner or later   15) utilized

Exercise 9: 1)～5) d   a   e   b   c

Exercise 10: 1)～5) B   C   B   C   D

Exercise 11: 1) He saw them off at the station last night.

2) I gave him a piece of advice.

3) I used to get up at six when I was at high school.

4) I am not going to stay here very long.

5) Mr. Brown is coming to have tea this afternoon.

Exercise 12:

Yesterday, I <u>didn't wake</u> up until 8:00 a.m. I <u>got</u> up immediately and <u>got</u> dressed. I <u>had</u> breakfast and <u>left</u> my house at 8:45. I <u>was</u> an hour late and <u>didn't get</u> to work until 9 o'clock. I <u>worked</u> all day and <u>didn't have</u> lunch. I <u>finished</u> working at 7:30 p.m. and <u>went</u> home at 8 p.m. I <u>was</u> two hours late and <u>didn't have</u> dinner until 9 o'clock. After dinner I <u>read</u> the newspaper for a while and <u>made</u> some telephone calls. I <u>listened</u> to the radio for two hours and <u>went</u> to bed at midnight. I <u>didn't go</u> to sleep immediately. I <u>slept</u> just six hours last night. I <u>didn't sleep</u> very well.

Unit 12

Exercise 1:

B: <u>It's difficult to learn</u>.

B: <u>Yes. But it's too difficult for me</u>.

B: <u>I see. Thank you very much</u>.

Exercise 2:

collection　　century　　professor　　imagine　　classics
fond　　　　afraid　　　personally　　relaxation　　excellent

Exercise 3: 1)～5) C　C　B　B　D

Exercise 4: 1) sentence　　2) beginner　　3) soon　　4) discovered　　5) west　　6) wisdom

　　　　　　7) volunteered　8) directions　9) essays　10) discussion　11) radiant

　　　　　　12) referred to　13) vast　　14) vest　　15) A suit of

Exercise 5: 1)～5) a　c　e　b　d

Exercise 6:

　　我迫切地想学说中国话，所以，我把我能买到的中文磁带和录像带全都买了下来，然后一遍又一遍地听，我和我的中国朋友们对话，并把我们的对话录下来。每天晚上，我都是听着这些磁带上床睡觉⋯就这样，我每天都要花四到五小时听说中文。

Exercise 7: 1)～5) C　A　A　D　C

Exercise 8: 1) circled　　2) vertical　3) underlined　4) appearance　5) margin　6) complicate

　　　　　　7) indicates　8) major　　9) marked　　10) in your mind　11) sequence

　　　　　　12) through　13) tied up　14) at the top of　15) fruitfully

Exercise 9: 1)～5) e　d　c　a　b

Exercise 10: 1)～6) B　B　D　A　B　A

Exercise 11: 1) All those people know English. What are they talking about?

　　　　　　2) I am waiting here for the bus. I always go to work by bus.

　　　　　　3) Look! It is raining again! Is it always raining at this time here?

　　　　　　4) The leader said that we would leave soon.

　　　　　　5) The foreign diplomats were to see the President.

Exercise 12:

　　My name is Walter. My sister's name is Mary and my brother's name is Leo. I speak French pretty well and a little Chinese.

　　Actually, my native language is English. I am studying French right now. my sister Mary is writing a letter to a friend of hers in South America. Her friend is an engineer. He speaks Spanish. He is studying English now but he doesn't speak English very well yet. I don't remember his name. At the moment, my brother Leo is reading a magazine. The magazine is in French. Leo reads French very well, and he speaks exceptionally well. Right now, I am thinking about my Chinese lesson. I have a lot of trouble with my pronunciation. I speak Chinese with an American accent.

Model Test 1

　　I. 1)～ 5) A　B　B　D　C　　　　　　6)～10) B　A　D　D　C

　　　11)～15) C　C　B　C　B

　　II. 16)～20) A　B　B　D　A　　　　　21)～25) C　B　A　B　B

　　　26)～30) D　A　B　A　A　　　　　31)～35) D　B　D　D　A

　　　36)～40) A　C　D　A　C　　　　　41)～45) D　A　B　B　A

III. 46)~50) B D B C A   51)~55) B   A   B   D   A

IV. 56)~60) A C C B A   61)~65) C   A   D   A   A

   66)~70) C B A B D   71)~75) B   A   D   B   C

V.

76）他们刚一到飞机场，老师就告诉他们这消息。（hardly…when）

77）学生花了两个半小时才做出这道数学题。（take）

78）我觉得现在为他的死而哭泣是没有用的。（no use）

79）作为一名中国人，我们应该把一生奉献给祖国。（devote…to）

80）我们上星期参观了这位科学家曾住过的房子。

81）She met that doctor.

82）He used to have a walk along the river.

83）Bicycles have many advantages.

84）She sings well, but also dances beautifully.

85）My parents keep encouraging me to study hard.

Model Test 2

I. 1)~ 5) B A C D C   6)~10) B   C   B   A   A

  11)~15) A A B C D

II. 16)~20) D A B A D   21)~25) C   C   D   B   A

   26)~30) C B A A B   31)~35) D   B   C   A   B

   36)~40) D C A A B   41)~45) D   A   D   D   C

III. 46)~50) A D A D D   51)~55) D   C   A   A   C

IV. 56)~60) C A B C D   61)~65) B   A   D   A   B

   66)~70) D C C A B   71)~75) A   B   B   D   C

V.

76）昨天我们用了大约两个小时做完了那件工作。

77）孩子们学好英语和计算机是很重要的。

78）上学期他学习不努力，结果数学考试不及格。

79）学生们对报告人所讲的内容很感兴趣。

80）当他们到达电影院时，电影已经开始了。

81）Beijing is one of the most beautiful cities she has visited.

82）They have lived in Beijing for many years.

83）Our wish will come true if we work hard.

84）The teacher told us that this novel was worth reading.

85）My friend asked me whether I had any difficulty in my work.